The Goat Farm

A Novel By

Rick Alan Rice

RARWRITER PUBLISHING GROUP

Dedicated to Joanne
(Anniversary 33)

Prologue

Pan has been with us from the beginning - Pan and the influence of Saturn, of which he is a shepherding moon. He is older than the Olympians, so old that his origins are clouded in mystery, though he is thought to be the son of Hermes, the psychopomp, the soul guide. The Greek tragedian Aeschylus suggested that he was the son of Zeus, or the son of Cronus.

Said to hail from Arcadia, in the Peloponnese, he was to the Greeks the god of the mountain wilderness, of shepherds and flocks, of music and spontaneous creativity. He provided Artemis with hunting dogs and taught prophecy to Apollo.

He was not worshiped in temples, but rather was a deity of the forests. His mother was the nymph Penelope of Mantinela.

He was a trickster. He wrapped himself in sheepskin to seduce the moon goddess Selene, luring her down from the sky and into his realm - the woods.

The Greeks saw him as a watcher, a guardian. He was the season of spring, the goat creature, consort to the nymphs, an embodiment of sexual energy.

He was the god of theatrical criticism, giving name to his review of human expression: *panic*.

The word *companion* comes from Pan, translating from the Ancient Greek to *all*.

The Greek historian Plutarch wrote of his death - he was believed to be the only god fated to a natural death - and of the deep sorrow that came over the world with news of his passing.

Saturn, however, did not stop broadcasting that message that it has always sent out through the universe. It is a message of liberation.

While Pan may no longer wander the woodlands, he is with us still.

He works through the elementals, conjured up from human thoughts, feelings, desires and impulses. It is they we now see in the trees, moving among the rocks and the undergrowth, navigating the dark passages, flitting among the branches and leaves.

They enter this world as the children of who we are, deep inside, and who he is - Pan, the creator.

They are our watchers, our guardians, ethereal extensions of ourselves that come to us in our dreams, and slip into our realities through the dark forest complexities of our human souls.

We are not all angels. We are nymphs and fairies, but also trolls, as ugly as we are beautiful. We are duality.

We breed disruption, our natural state, and in the midst of our ongoing, self-created conflict we yearn for someone we can turn to, perhaps a father or a mother figure.

And we conflict with the creatures of Gaia - those associated with certain places, and with the subterranean world. They intervene, involve themselves in our vast confusion.

And so we dream of peace from our own madness, knowing that peace is itself a dream, for the governing of our elemental selves requires sensitivities beyond the reach of most.

It is a woman's job. That is Pan's irony.

And governing Pan's chaotic creations requires a certain kind of female spirit.

CHAPTER 1

"Seriously, Joanna, you think Hillary Clinton would have created order from chaos?"

Grinning, Ben glanced quickly at her, sitting next to him in the passenger seat, watching the road ahead like a hawk. Driving along Highway 174 was a twisting, turning challenge, and he didn't dare take his eyes off the road for long. Neither did she.

"Yeah, well, sue me, but I think we need a woman president," said Joanna, bracing into a turn.

"You mean just for form's sake, because its past time it happened?" asked Ben.

"That and women are just smarter than men, everybody knows that."

Ben grinned. "There have been plenty of female leaders down through history, and it is not apparent to me that they have been any less screwed up than their male counterparts. Remember Margaret Thatcher? Or how about Theresa May, for Christ sakes!"

"Fuck the British, they're always idiots," said Joanna.

"Language, language," said Ben. "Vulgarities never help."

Joanna looked at him askance, while intuitively grabbing for the seldom-used hand strap above the passenger door, leveraging as the car careened into the next set of slalom curves. "Sometimes they do, like if someone is doing something you want them to stop doing, you say 'knock it the fuck off' and they stop right away. They get that you are serious, because you said fuck."

"That is fucking stupid," Ben muttered, shaking his head, involuntarily bumping it once against the driver's side window as he wrenched the car through an S-curve in the road.

"No its not," said Joanna.

"Yes it is."

"No its not, and you're stupid for not even voting," said Joanna, gripping the dash. "Slow the fuck down!"

"Well, when someone stands up a good woman – and I don't count Hillary Clinton in that category – then I'll be the first to cast my ballot," said Ben, rather enjoying the roller coaster ride, maybe speeding up a little.

"What woman would you vote for?" asked Joanna, eyes wide, staring into the uncertainty of their near future, just the next turn away.

"The kind with a firm handle on just who she is, not one thinking her whole life that she is one kind of exotic flower, when really she's another," said Ben, with an ornery grin.

"Exotic flower?" asked Joanna, glancing out into the passing trees of the forest, trying to imagine.

"Well, yeah, you know, like you think you are Portuguese, like all the beautiful fashion models are, but it turns out you are French," said Ben, "like women with hairy arm pits. That has to be tough."

Joanna slugged him on the arm, causing Ben to fake mutter - "Ouch, I'm driving here."

He had been giving her a tough time ever since an Ancestor DNA test revealed that she was fully one-third French. She grew up in a household with one grandmother speaking Portuguese, the other Italian, and nobody ever said anything about having any relatives in France. This struck Ben as particularly funny because Joanna's mother had been a proud Portuguese woman and Joanna had grown up participating in their ethnic festivals and parades. She had even been a Portuguese Festival Princess in her youth. As it turned out, she could have been just as justified celebrating Bastille Day, or parading around as Joan of Arc.

They had been married forever, or that's what Ben always said. "A hundred years" was always his best guess, though it had really only been thirty-three. Ben was now sixty-six, and Joanna sixty-five.

They never had children, though that had not been a planned thing, but rather just something that never happened for them. It had never really been an issue. Joanna had been afraid of the idea of giving birth, and Ben spent most of his time lost in his own world anyway. A life of the mind. He was a novelist who had managed to get a few things published, but nothing ever sold well enough to do anything more than recoup the costs of the bombs he created. He had a literary agent who hung with him, thinking one day Ben might write something that would bring in some money. Ben, however, had to rely on technical writing jobs to pay the bills.

Joanna had worked in sales, when she was young, and later in education, but she had never been particularly motivated by any of that, and she never made any money herself. Together, she and Ben were trolling the bottom side of California's poverty-stricken "middle class", until Joanna's mother died and left her a small fortune, which she hoped would be enough to buy the home she always wanted.

Joanna had been conceived at South Lake Tahoe and the Sierra-Nevada range held a strong appeal for her, even though her lungs could no longer handle anything over a 2,500-foot elevation. She had been smoking a pack of cigarettes a day since she was fifteen, so her level of oxygen utilization was poor. It was a testimony to her grit that she was even still alive.

In fact, she was not only alive but amazingly well preserved. She was pretty, petite, brunette without a touch of gray, and naturally vivacious, with beautiful dark eyes and a fine jaw line.

Time hadn't been as kind to Ben. He was thin-to-bald on top, and paunchy in the middle. Where in his youth he had been an agile and athletic lad, with long, flowing blond hair and reasonably good features, he now looked like an old insurance salesman, which in his eyes was as bad as things could get. The deterioration had done a job on his sense of self and destroyed what might have remained of any intimacy he might have had left to express. The sex had all gone out of him, not necessarily her.

CHAPTER 2

"Are you scared?"

Ben was always posing this question to Joanna, mostly as a taunt. She did this thing where she would start making a nervous sound when they would drive on what she perceived to be a dangerous road. The Sierra back country is filled with them, roads where the pavement suddenly stops and then there is only rutted dirt to drive along. The foliage closes in on either side and the light disappears, blotted out by the tree canopy that closes over the trail and threatens to consume you whole. The forest feels alive, shimmering in the breeze, shining with reflected sunlight that comes and goes, burbling with seasonal streams and water cascades. There are deer everywhere, and foxes and cougars and bears. You don't see the latter much, but they are there in number, seemingly growing more pervasive every year, as human development has imposed itself on their territories.

Ben talks constantly about Bigfoot, which he believes to be a real thing. He has this fantasy that he will move to a place in the Sierras and somehow encounter the creature and communicate with him. It's the kind of nutty thing Ben says these days, which has had Joanna a little worried. Is it possible that he is going senile at sixty-six?

They only met in their early thirties, after each had been around the block a few times. Joanna had traveled extensively, been everywhere, and was ready to settle down. Ben had wandered out from the Midwest with every expectation of having a successful writing career on the west coast. That had kind of happened, but certainly not in the way that he had wanted. He had depended upon mundane documentation projects, which he did as a contractor, to support his writing habit, which was obsessive. He would spend hours each day just typing away, writing down anything that came into his head.

Joanna had never been a fan of her husband's writing, but she had been a fan of his sense of humor and his stability. He was the same guy every day, and not bad in any way. He was of sufficient size that he had been able to make her feel safe and protected, and his income had helped give them a level of financial security. Things, however, were changing. Time was taking its toll, especially on Ben, and Joanna now didn't feel as protected by him as she once had, which is part of why these mountain roads made her nervous.

The Sierras had become filled with pot growers the way that the northern California counties had been before the state liberalized its marijuana laws. A person can get into trouble really fast by wandering down the wrong trail, and then there are the militias, and the State of Jefferson. Ben and Joanna had stumbled upon one property where someone had strung a large banner across the road reading BUILD THE WALL AND CRIME WILL FALL. The preponderance of American flags told them they could get shot just by being in the area, so they had back-tracked fast.

*

At the end of the long dirt road, they finally reached the property. There was a gated entrance, with a metal frame structure that arched over the entryway above the swinging, metal gate. Rusted, metal-crafted letters proclaimed: "The Goat Farm".

"Wow, this is it," said Ben. "It doesn't look like anyone is here."

"I thought Maria called the agent," said Joanna.

"Yeah, she did," said Ben. "She didn't say if the house would be open, and she didn't mention anything about a gate. Do you suppose I should just open it and drive in?"

From where they sat, debating what to do, they could see the two-story farmhouse that, to them, looked like it belonged in the French countryside. It was sky blue with white trim, that included crafted window and door treatments, and a charming balcony off the second-floor bedrooms.

"The Nazis will be occupying this place." That was Ben's comment when he first saw the house. Joanna was one of the few people in the world who could ever comprehend her husband's cryptic allusions, which may have had something to do with why his books never sold. If the Nazis were going to occupy it, it must look to Ben to be French – that was the kind of disambiguation he required, and Joanna had developed the skills of a Turing code breaker in his regard.

Ben got out and opened the gate, and then got back in and drove the car into the yard. It was all dirt. There was a beautiful and large California Black Walnut tree that had the effect of creating a circular drive in front of the house. Guarding this area was a rusted metal sculpture of the Hindu Goddess Kali.

"Okay, that's interesting," Ben said, as he brought the car to a halt. It was an understatement, as the sculpture was at least eight feet tall and a little intimidating. It was like a scarecrow for keeping people away, or such was the feeling it seemed to evince, though in Tantric sects Kali is worshiped as a divine protector who bestows liberation, not fear. Ben was unaware.

He and Joanna got out of the car and looked around.

The property stretched in all directions, and included a number of out-buildings, including a good-sized barn, several stalls and paddocks for keeping animals, and an elaborate and secured section of irrigated soil.

The area was largely overgrown in tall green grass, and it was a rustic setting, with weathered wood fencing, rusted metal pen gates, and rusted aluminum shed roofs.

Besides the house, the most prominent feature was a lagoon that was situated about thirty yards from the house's back side. There a redwood deck had been constructed, along with a canvas cover from the sun.

The lagoon was of significant size, with what appeared to be a floating island in its middle, and it was the first feature Joanna visited. While she walked down the little path to the water, Ben stepped up onto the front porch of the house, where he found a white cardboard sign, hanging by twine from the doorknob, that read: "Open – don't lock".

This was curious. Their realtor Maria typically accompanied them on these look-see types of visits, because she was approved with the local realtor association and so had the combinations to the keypad locks that typically hung from doors of the houses they would visit. Why this one didn't work that way was a mystery, as was the reason Maria had given about not accompanying them to view the place. For whatever reason, she didn't seem to want to have anything to do with it, though she had called the realtor who listed the property to get approval for Ben and Joanna to visit. They had assumed that meant that someone would be there to meet them, show them around, and let them into the house.

Nothing was as expected.

Ben saw the sign hanging from the doorknob and let himself inside to look around.

He was a little surprised by what he saw there.

Everywhere he looked, there was either Hindu, Christian, or occult imagery, or there was strange artwork depicting demons, unidentifiable human forms, tortured faces, and UFOs. The image of Ganesha - the remover of obstacles, the patron of arts and sciences, and the deva of intellect and wisdom, the god of beginnings – was prominent, but there were also pentagrams, wicker men, and a horned skull, covered with red enamel paint, that bothered Ben immediately. It was an odd stew of spirit influences, and not at all what he was expecting to find in the French farmhouse of his imagination.

"How does it look?"

Joanna appeared at the door, having checked out the lagoon. "Oooh, I like it," she purred as she started wandering around the first floor of the house, which had clearly been put together by a "creative". That's what they call them in San Francisco, anyway: people who have ideas outside of the reactive. They have become so rare that they are now informally classified as a unique human type, at least in the area from which Ben and Joanna were escaping.

The creative living in this place had painted the walls artfully in deep natural forest shades of green, brown and maroon.

"It doesn't have a jetted tub," said Ben. That was always one of the first things they checked, because Joanna had put a high premium on a therapeutic wash.

"I don't care, I like it," said Joanna.

And that was it. After months of driving around the Sierras, touring houses and arguing over what they wanted and needed in their new home, Joanna made a snap decision.

"I like it too," Ben said, "but I haven't even looked around the property. Check out the artwork in this house. I'm going to go walk around."

Ben walked down to the lagoon and looked at the water, noticing that it did not appear brackish in the way he expected, but rather was clean to the extent that he could see several feet into its depths. The bank fell away so that he couldn't see the bottom, but the setting was fresh. There was an island in the middle, where the grass grew tall, as it did all around the lagoon, though not so much on that side where the deck had been constructed. There was no apparent source for the water that was feeding this lagoon, prompting Ben to assume that there must be an underground stream.

He then walked over to the paddock area, where there was a row of open, covered stalls, all with fresh hay in them, and a sign that read "Goat Crossing". Other than within the pens, the place was overgrown with tall green grass. California had experienced an unusually rainy winter, pulling the state out of drought conditions, and now the Golden State looked like Ireland, almost surrealistically beautiful in its vivid display. Here at the Goat Farm colors seemed to pop, to practically come alive with radiance. Ben imagined that he could smell the color green.

On the far side of the property, he found a medium-sized barn, a classic wooden frame structure that had been weatherized with an aluminum roof. Inside were eight stalls, also fresh with hay, though there was no sign that animals had been kept there any time recently. He looked up at the rafters, trying to assess the condition of the barn, and it seemed solid – dark, actually, in the area where the roof peaked, signaling that it was well sealed, not even light getting through.

Ben walked around behind the barn, where he expected to find a meadow area, based on a satellite photo he had studied. There he found it, shielded behind a wall of tall weeds. Pushing through, he viewed an open area at the edge of the forest that appeared to have been recently mowed or maintained in some way. He didn't walk in but, looking at the meadow from the perimeter, he surmised that it must have been used as grazing land for the goats that had roamed the property.

He crossed all the way back to the house – Joanna was still lost inside, exploring the home's nooks and crannies – and then wandered around to the other side and up a path he found there. It led to another group of outbuildings, and there he found a fenced area where there was an elevated sprinkler system. White PVC tubing was raised to a height of about one foot above the soil, set up in a matrix pattern to cover an area of perhaps sixty-feet square.

"Wow," Ben muttered to himself, imagining the garden one might plant in this specially prepared area.

He stepped across a threshold into the planting area and instantly a light came on. He looked up to see a security camera mounted to the side of a small house trailer, along with a sign that read: "You are on camera". And immediately, Ben sensed that he had trespassed into an area that had no doubt been used for growing marijuana. There were clearly no plants there at this time, and the growers were gone, but the fact that there was a camera there, that appeared to be working, creeped him out. Ben wondered if somewhere there was someone watching him on a monitor.

12

CHAPTER 3

Joanna was hooked.

"I like it Ben," she said. "I think this is the one, let's take it!"

Just like her, he thought. She had fallen in love with properties before, but then the next day changed her mind when she started thinking more deeply about them, so Ben had learned not to put much credence in her first reaction to anything.

"I like it," he said, allowing that "it's a strange place…"

"That's what I like about it," said Joanna.

"I feel like I need to know more about it," said Ben. "Where is the owner? Why are they selling? And why is it so dead around here? When was it last actively used as a goat farm? Not that I can imagine what that even means. Do they milk these things, sell goat milk?" he asked, shaking his head.

"Or rent them out for grazing," said Joanna. "Remember that herd of goats we used to see all the time around Benicia? I think the city rented them to maintain city land. Maybe these people did something like that, renting out their herd."

"I feel like it would be a good thing to talk to the neighbor and see what they could tell us about the property," said Ben.

"Sure, if you want to," said Joanna.

"You want to drive up the road and see if we can talk to someone?"

Joanna shook her head. "No, you go. I want to spend a little time thinking about what I could do with this place."

"Well, okay – I'll shut the gate behind me," said Ben. "You going to be okay here by yourself?"

"Yeah, I'll be fine," said Joanna, already preoccupied with her decorating ideas.

*

The only other property on the road to the Goat Farm was about a half-mile away, and not visible from the farm. The Goat Farm itself was situated on undulating land, not a flat, and there was a high, forested hill between the farm and the next property.

Ben pulled into the yard of the neighboring farmer – he assumed that he would be a farmer, of some kind – and brought his car to a stop in the yard in front of the house. It was a typical arrangement, with a dirt turnaround in front of a farmhouse with a fenced yard. There were two mean-looking German Shepherds in a heavy-duty cage at the far side of the yard, and they went crazy when they saw Ben, leaping against the wire mesh enclosure like they wanted to tear him apart. It was intimidating and as Ben approached the house he wondered if dropping in unannounced was a wise idea.

There was a screened front door, but otherwise the house seemed to be open, though it was dark. Ben couldn't see inside. He walked up onto the covered porch and the dogs went insane, violently shaking their enclosure. He looked over at them nervously, half-expecting that someone inside the house would trigger a release on the door of that cage and suddenly those two giant Alsatians would be on him. Ben was afraid of dogs, and particularly these kinds of dogs, which he knew had killed more people than any other breed. The two of them could tear him apart in less than a minute.

Losing his nerve, he looked back at the screen door, wondering if he should knock, or just slink away, when a voice from inside the house said - "What do you want? What are you doing on my property?"

Ben froze for a moment. He could hear in the tone of this disembodied voice that he was not welcome. He kept glancing at those dogs, fully expecting to see them flying toward him from that cage. They acted crazy, like they hadn't been fed in a long time.

He looked at the screen door, which was just dark. "Am I okay with your dogs?" he asked nervously. "I don't want to get bit."

"Then got off my fuckin' porch," said the voice.

"I'm sorry to just show up like this," said Ben, frantically glancing from the screen door to the dog cage. "I was wondering about the property up the road."

As soon as he said that, a big man appeared at the door. He towered above Ben. Bearded, weathered, and hardened from decades of toil in tough conditions, he did not appear to be of the same human line from which Ben had descended, and he was not friendly. "I don't want nothin' to do with you people, now get off my property."

"I don't know anything about who has lived on that place up the road, I am just trying to find out..."

"Get off my fucking property," said the big man menacingly. "I don't know anything about those people up there, or what goes on at that property, and I don't want to, now get the hell out of here or those dogs are coming free."

CHAPTER 4

The experience with the neighbor scared the shit out of Ben and convinced him that the Goat Farm was not for him. He tried to imagine what it would be like sharing maintenance duties on this private road with a neighbor who wanted to have his dogs tear him apart. That was not the dynamic that he was yearning to leave the Bay Area for.

"That did not go well," he told Joanna, but it didn't seem to faze her at all. She had fallen in love with the place. It was as if she was transfixed, and it was confusing to Ben because this ridiculous farm property had been his fantasy, not hers. Now she was the one who was enamored with it, while Ben felt every inclination to run away.

"Seriously, you think this is the place?" asked Ben.

"I know it is," said Joanna, "I can feel it. I feel like I belong here."

"On the Goat Farm?" asked Ben, incredulous. "You feel like the Goat Farm is right for you? I have never heard you say you had any interest in living on a farm. I can't even get you to go with me to visit relatives in Nebraska, and you want to live on this goat farm?"

"Yes," said Joanna, eyes wide as she looked at everything around her. "I can't explain it, it takes me by surprise, too, but I love it here."

So, it was decided that they would have a conversation with the realtor who had listed the property, and even that proved to be strange.

Ben called Mountain Properties Realty and a man answered. He had one of those flat, lifeless, uninflected voices that indicated that he either hated his job or was just unbelievably bored with it. "Hi, I am interested in that property up on Hill Point, and I understand that you have that listing."

"That is correct," said the man. "That property is a former goat farm that is being sold as is, no contingencies or negotiations. The price is set and will not be adjusted. It is a cash-only deal. We do not arrange financing."

Ben listened quietly for a moment, letting that sink in.

"Well, okay, that being the case, I would like to speak with the owner before offering to meet the listed price," said Ben. "Would it be possible to set up a meeting?"

"Be at my office at ten o'clock tomorrow morning," said the voice, and before Ben could say a thing the agent hung up.

*

The conversation with the real estate agent felt about as good to Ben as did the conversation with his only neighbor. "I don't know, Joanna," he told his wife. "I like this property but there is some kind of a vibe about this whole place. Something about it bothers me, and it bothers the neighbor. The owner seems remote, to say the least, and the real estate agent is downright rude. What is going on?"

"I don't know, but I love it here, and I wish you would go talk to the realtor and see what he wants for it," said Joanna.

"I already know what he wants for it," said Ben. "It is exactly the price listed, no room for negotiation, sold as is. That's the deal. I don't know when the roof was last replaced, or anything about the septic tank, or the propane, or the maintenance cost on this ten-acre property. I know nothing."

"So go find out, talk to the agent," said Joanna.

"Don't you have questions?" asked Ben. "Don't you want to come along?"

"No," said Joanna, looking around the house like a kid at Christmas. "There is nothing more that I need to know."

*

That was some kind of a sign, right there. Their entire marriage, Joanna had been a control freak. She controlled their finances and was generally an impossible person to steer in any direction not of her own choosing. She had never trusted Ben with money, even his own, so this idea that he alone deal with the real estate agent and speak to the property owner was completely out of character for her.

Ben was thinking about this the next morning as he opened the door to the realtor's office. It was 9:59 a.m., so he was right on time.

He walked in to find an office that appeared to be no longer in use. There were no lights on, no receptionist there to greet anyone, and the accumulation of dust on the ancient wood furnishings told him no one had occupied this space for a long time.

Just when he was about to back on out, assuming he had entered the wrong building, the dark form of a man appeared in a doorway on the far side of the room. It was a tall, wiry figure whose form brought to mind an undertaker out of Hollywood's golden era of classic horror, like a spirit animated by the memory of Karloff or Lugosi.

The form in the doorway motioned him to come his way, then withdrew from sight into the room that he beckoned Ben towards.

With no small trepidation, Ben crossed the waiting area to the doorway where the realtor had stood for a moment before disappearing.

The boards of the old hardwood floor creaked under his feet with each step - the only sounds in the place. It was a funereal environment, not at all like any active business he had ever been in. It was dead energy.

"Have a seat," said the realtor as Ben entered the room.

There sat an old woman with long white hair, looking worn and haggard and a lot like an ancient witch. She didn't acknowledge Ben's presence as he walked into the room.

"Hello," said Ben, extending his hand in greeting.

The old woman glanced up at him and nodded, but she didn't accept his offer of a handshake.

"Mrs. Breedlove, this gentleman is interested in buying your property," said the realtor flatly.

"Yes, I am," said Ben, "but I think first I need to know a little bit more about it." He paused to judge her reaction, but when there was none he continued. "Have you lived there long?"

"Yes," said the old lady.

Ben glanced over at the realtor, who looked down at the papers on his desk, not making eye contact.

"I understand it was a goat farm," said Ben.

"Yes," said Mrs. Breedlove.

"How recently has it been actively used in that way?" asked Ben.

"Recently," said the old lady.

Again, Ben stayed silent for a moment, hoping Mrs. Breedlove would take up the challenge and be more forthcoming with information, but she said nothing, just looked down at the floor before the chair on which she sat.

"May I ask why you have decided to sell the property?" asked Ben.

The lady then looked at him, and he could see in her eyes that she was old and exhausted. "I can't do it anymore, it's time to give it up," she said, her voice quivering. "I had my kids there, gone now, like my husband." And she added – "He's gone below, where the goblins go."

Ben started to smile, thinking she might be referencing a line from The Wizard of Oz, signaling an unexpected sense of humor, or hidden personality, but the look in her eyes told him otherwise.

He glanced over at the realtor, who was still avoiding eye contact, looking down at his papers.

"So, you want the property?" he asked, without looking up.

22

CHAPTER 5

Joanna had been having this recurring dream in which she didn't have to be afraid.

She had been afraid her whole life, which had been characterized by eating disorders and anxiety issues. While young, she had gotten a first-class birth on the pharmacy train. That was back when doctors were passing out Alprazolam to the chemically unbalanced suffering from panic and depression. Taking it became a life sentence, a one-way ticket to jangle town, after which being without it was even worse. Joanna lived in constant fear of being unable to re-fill ancient prescriptions written over the years by doctors who probably thought they were helping. She particularly dreaded and resented the way the medical community treated her like an addict each time she had to introduce herself to a new general practitioner. Sometimes the enormity of it all paralyzed her. She worried that she wasn't pleasing people and was constantly under the impression that she had done something wrong, even though she didn't know what it was. She would feel constant concern that Ben was mad at her for one reason or another, and she often expressed guilt over situations she had no control over whatsoever.

Control, in fact, was at the root of her issue. She had to feel in control to feel any level of ease at all.

Astrologically, Joanna was a bull. Numerologically, she was an "8", the number symbolizing the principle of domination. She felt compelled to perform the responsibilities of an executive decision-maker while feeling conflicted about acting in that way, pushed in one direction to be Joan of Arc while pulled in another to avoid common reality as if it were poison. It was neutralizing to the extent that she had become a little reclusive over the years. She engaged with life for only as long as it took to meet her basic obligations, and then she retreated to her room where she would sit and smoke, staring ahead as if in a stupor.

She would never admit it, but Ben had saved her. Left to her own devices, she had been bound to struggle, caught in her inner conflict. In fact, she had been furious to learn that her father had once confided to Ben's father that Ben had "saved my daughter". Joanna didn't need any fucking saving, and in this dream she kept having this was the prominent feature.

She was walking across a deep gorge – so deep that when she looked down, she couldn't see the bottom – and all she had below her feet was a thin rope no thicker than dental floss.

She was wearing ballerina slippers. Pink.

In the dream, she felt no fear.

She would bounce on the tiny filament, daring it to break, to fail and allow her to fall, with full confidence that would not happen. This all happened to the audible gasps and horrors of onlookers. There were people in her dream, faceless voices who were watching, and she delighted in horrifying them, turning pirouettes on her little tightrope above this descent that fell away with cartoon perspective, narrowing rapidly at the bottom so that it looked impossibly far below.

She would leap in the air and turn a flip, then lightly settle back down on her little gorge string, which would sag and sway, and none of it bothered her in the least, though those watching sounded like they were having heart attacks. "Somebody save her!" she would hear somebody yell, but she didn't need any saving, she felt free. It felt as if she owned the natural world, as if it was impossible for gravity or even her own fear to make her fall.

Then she would wake up and it would be hard to fill her lungs with air, and she would feel the panic come with a new day.

In her mind, she had concocted this elaborate fantasy in which that new day never hurt, but rather was a welcomed joy, a new opportunity for her to feel that never-ending control of all those things that vexed her.

Up in the Sierras she would feel differently than she always had on her home turf in the Bay Area. Up in the elevation and the fresh air it felt to her like being on vacation, a feeling no doubt engendered by the many vacations she had taken with her family to this area when she was a girl.

Hell, she had been conceived in Tahoe.

The granite cordillera called out to her with a promise of freedom from whatever it was that made it hard for her to be happy.

That and Lita Breedlove's skull.

26

CHAPTER 6

"You got to be fucking kidding me, man! We are never going to get this truck up this funky-ass dirt road!"

There had been no talking Joanna out of it, she wanted the Goat Farm, and so they paid cash for the property and the deal was done. They hired a trio of movers to load up their home in the Bay Area and transport it to the front range of the Sierras, where they ran into all kinds of problems. Their truck was almost too wide to make it across the two narrow bridges they encountered along the dirt road leading to the property. They had to position a guy on the ground on either side of the truck to direct the driver across so that he didn't drop a wheel off one side or the other. The tree canopy was so low that the truck snapped off limbs as it crept along the road, leafy branches falling down around and onto the hood of the truck as they moved, lurching left and right as they encountered deep ruts, one after the next.

"What kind of a fuckin' idiot would live back here?" asked Dominion. He was their leader, a former gang banger who had spent time in the California penal system for selling marijuana back in the day when that was a crime. He was in his forties now and still a fit Black man and the supervisor of a crew of two other younger Black dudes. One was quiet and introverted, and the other a real Mandingo – a mixed martial arts fighter and a professional boxer who had moved to California from St. Louis to work as a trainer. That hadn't gone well, so now he was moving furniture for Dominion.

"We gonna break a damned axle driving back into this shithole," said Dominion. "Why these crazy fuckin' White people want to haul all this shit way back in here?"

The three of them would volunteer that they were not at all comfortable there in the backwoods. You almost never saw Black people in that area, and that alone made them feel unwelcome. And then there were the surroundings.

The drive up to the Goat Farm was like a passage to another dimension, one filled with sight and sound, like the Twilight Zone, except that all the elements in play were natural. The breeze moving through the trees seemed to carry voices, like invisible children playing and laughing, and the sounds of birds echoed with great stereophonic effect, as if in a sound chamber. The aroma wafting through the trees was intoxicating, inducing something close to a dream state.

All three movers were potheads, but Dominion was adamant about no one smoking on the job. Moving along the road to the Goat Farm, it didn't feel like they needed any further sedation, the area itself feeling drugged.

They started seeing things.

"Did you see that?" One of them asked.

Dominion's eyes were big as saucers. Yeah, he saw that. It looked like a curly-headed kid running alongside of them through the forest, which was impossible, because the forest was so thick with undergrowth that a person could hardly walk through it, let alone run.

"What in the fuck was that?" said the quiet one, who wasn't about to admit it, but he was also the spooky one. "Did you see that?" he asked, glancing at his coworkers with a panicked expression.

"I didn't see nothing," volunteered Dominion, keeping his eyes on the road.

"I saw something," said the fighter. "I don't think it was a person."

"I'm talking about that kid!" said the quiet one to Dominion, alarmed. "You didn't see that?" He craned his neck to look out the open window on the passenger side. "I don't see him now, but that fucker was leaping through the forest like a wild animal. I'm talking about a kid! Did you see that?"

"I didn't see nothing," said Dominion, staring ahead.

When they reached the second narrow bridge, the quiet one and the fighter got out of the truck to help Dominion steer the truck across. It was tight, tighter than the first bridge they came to. Dominion began to worry about what would happen were they to get back in here with all this furniture, but then not be able to get back out. That struck him as totally conceivable, and panic began to grow in his mind.

They had only just gotten the truck over the little wooden bridge when they heard the sound of dogs barking. Dominion glanced in his side mirror and in the distance, closing fast, were two enormous German Shepherds.

"Get in the fuckin' truck!" he yelled.

His two workers looked back and saw the dogs approaching and they scrambled to get to the passenger side door and safety. They only just got the door shut when the dogs attacked from both sides. The guys got the windows rolled up just in time to keep the animals from leaping into the cab with them. One of the dogs ripped the side-view mirror from the passenger side mount, while the other snarled and bit at Dominion through the window glass on the driver's side, his teeth clattering against the pane.

Dominion hit the gas and the truck lurched ahead up the road, contents leaping and jumping in the back, fragile objects breaking, as he picked up speed on the deteriorated roadway to put distance between them and the dogs.

In the driver's side mirror, Dominion saw a large man appear on the road behind them and fire a shotgun up into the air. The dogs suddenly stopped their attack and went back to where he stood on the road, watching the movers disappear further up the mountain trail.

*

For whatever reason, Mrs. Breedlove never returned to the Goat Farm to remove any of what she had left behind. She abandoned it all: furniture, housewares, wall art, everything but the few personal items she had taken with her when she had abandoned the farm months earlier.

In researching the property, Ben found that her last recorded contact with any governing authority was in the missing person's report she had filed years earlier after the disappearance of her husband. They had apparently not lived there long before she lost him.

Ben didn't find this in his research, but her report had just been an effort to create some sort of a cover story for what had happened, for she knew full well where he had gone.

She had no guilt in the matter, nothing for which to be absolved. The Goat Farm had simply done what the Goat Farm had always done, and now he was gone and she was alone, and years had passed and now she was done with it. She had done her part, brought a period of order to the chaos that was the natural state of the place, and now it was time for someone else to take the burden, to care for the kids.

It was time for someone else to make that sacrifice.

CHAPTER 7

Joanna could not stop looking at the red skull.

It is "just so fucking weird", is what she was thinking if one could hear.

It looked like someone had found this elongated skull and used fingernail polish – many bottles of fingernail polish – to cover the whole thing in this overwhelming carnal red. Why would someone do that? Or more to the point, what kind of a *person* would do that?

This wasn't artful in any way, it was just shocking. It was as if the thing had been created for effect.

Who would do that?

Joanna sat in a living room chair, holding the skull in her two hands, asking all these questions. She explored each nook and cranny of this perfectly preserved artifact, and she tried to imagine what this thing must have looked like in life. Now it just looked like a flayed creature; maybe like what this thing looked like just after its skin was first peeled away.

It had to be a goat and must have come from right here, she reasoned – the Goat Farm. Someone had found this skull and then decided to cover it in red lacquer?

Why would there be a skeletal goat lying around the property? Surely the previous owners had cared enough about their animals that they hadn't just let them die and decompose to skeletal remains. Who would do that?

"Where did you come from?" Joanna asked the skull aloud, and she had no sooner uttered the question than she heard the answer.

Was that in her mind?

"The meadow."

For a moment, Joanna froze as she processed the voice she heard, which seemed present, as if it was in the room, and she suddenly startled and quickly set the skull down on the floor in front of her.

She instinctively cupped her hands over her face, covering her nose and mouth, so only her eyes revealed her shock.

She glanced quickly around the room – nothing there – and then back at the skull.

And then she let out an amazed, relieved laugh.

Joanna loved horror. She loved the books, the movies, the horrible headlines. For someone who had a chipper personality – Ben met her right after some higher up in the organization she worked for had dubbed her "Chipper Monkey" – Joanna had a dark streak. She seemed to find terror in others entertaining, which was utterly at odds with her behavioral nature, which was unremittingly empathetic. She was, in a sense, a perfect balance of Yen/Yang suffering, rather like Lucifer, the enlightened.

Joanna looked down at the skull, resting between her feet, looking up at her.

"You seem mighty sure of yourself," Joanna muttered.

She had noticed that about this goat – this skull without skin or muscle. He seemed happy with himself, like he was grinning.

"You think the ewe is ready, don't you, you old fucker," Joanna said knowingly to the skull

"I doubt he was fucking ewes," said Ben, who unrecognized by Joanna had come upon the scene and taken up a vantage point, leaning against a doorway. "Male goats have sex with does and nannys. Ewes are sheep women."

"He'd fuck a sheep, I can tell," said Joanna, still staring at the skull.

"Well, who wouldn't?" said Ben, matter-of-factly.

Joanna didn't take her eyes off the skull. "That does that, we're not getting any sheep."

"Just joking," said Ben, "I wouldn't really fuck a sheep."

"How about a goat?" asked Joanna.

Ben shook his head. "No, I wouldn't be a goat fucker, either. I'm not into sex with animals. How about you?"

"I suppose it depends on the animal," said Joanna drolly, though her attentions were totally focused on this horrible skull.

It looked at her, sighting her beautiful face between her knees.

The fucker looked confident.

34

CHAPTER 8

Ben was dreading their first night in the house. He had trouble sleeping at any rate, and always struggled in an unfamiliar environment.

Throughout their entire marriage, Joanna had been a nut for horror novels and scary movies. While she had a fine sense for what was crap, and what was sublime, she consumed all of it with a voracity that baffled Ben. He found all that minorly entertaining, but schlock horror was not his thing.

The truth of the matter was that he didn't have the constitution for it. Gross violence upset him, even to read about. He had such a wild imagination that any little suggestion of weirdness could cascade into a full-blown living nightmare for him. He tended to feel ashamed of his own inability to control his panic, which he felt revealed an immaturity in him that would follow him to the grave, if that was possible. Ben was afraid of the dark.

They had no media services and only barely had cell phone coverage.

Ben and Joanna had resigned themselves to the fact that they were going to have to rely on satellite services for television and internet, and none of that was in place yet. This was a big psychological hurdle for them, because Joanna had once worked for one of the premium cable services and they had become used to having the whole entertainment package: the movies and the niche programming, like Ben's beloved "Ancient Aliens". Moving to the

Goat Farm was going to reset their entire sense of media reality, though that first night they could only speculate as to what that might mean. They picked up an FM radio signal and left it on for a full hour before realizing it was a religious broadcaster sermonizing with a pop music indistinguishable from secular strains, outside of references to the Lord.

Joanna drank Bloody Marys while Ben nursed a bottle of Carnivor, a cabernet he had grown attached to. And, of course, they smoked pot.

Smoking pot had been the thing that brought them together. It revealed that what they had in common were cultural references, including a shared feeling of absolute certainty that pot smokers were the best of human kind. At least stoners tended to be light-hearted, and as both knew alcohol to have the opposite effect they found common bond with the notion that pot was pure. Smoking together became a communal experience, a reaffirmation of the fact that they got one another. And so that just went on and on, for years, functioning as the central thread that held their marriage together, this complete commitment to being stoned out of their minds.

It was getting them through that first night, which was rough.

Joanna remained absorbed with futzing with the interior, arranging and hanging things.

"You aren't planning on keeping the red horned skull, I hope," said Ben, who could hardly look at the thing. It just scared him, for some reason, like the type of thing one might innocently hang in one's house not knowing that it was inviting a visit from the devil himself.

"I wish we had TV," Ben muttered to himself. "Or even Alexa."

Amazon Alexa didn't work, of course. Ben had purchased one of the devices for Joanna the previous Christmas, and it turned out to be the gift that kept on giving until they moved out of internet range and Alexa went stupid.

"Do you know that we don't have a CD player?" asked Joanna. "How can we not have a fuckin' CD player?"

"Language," pleaded Ben. "You are not a longshoreman."

"Well, I'm a farmer now," countered Joanna. "I bet they all cuss like stevedores."

Ben frowned. "Do you know stevedores to be foul mouthed?"

"Oh sure, they're filthy with the lingo," said Joanna, continuing her futzing.

Ben rolled his eyes and went back to sipping his wine, glancing nervously at the windows all around. "You know, it is so easy for me to imagine sitting here in the living room and looking up and seeing Bigfoot staring in at me from the porch."

"I'm sure you'd love that," said Joanna, paying no real attention.

"I'd shit my pants," said Ben. "I like the idea of him more than the idea of having him look at me from just outside the very thin walls of this house."

Joanna dropped something in the kitchen and Ben leaped about a foot off the sofa. "What was that?" he asked.

"Relax, I just dropped something," said Joanna from the next room. "Did you think Bigfoot had you?"

"No," said Ben, sounding none too convincing.

This went on until after midnight, when Joanna decided she was ready to try going to sleep.

"I guess we might know by now if this place is haunted," said Ben, in all seriousness.

"It doesn't feel haunted," said Joanna, not at all concerned.

Ben felt a shiver run up his back, all the way to his neck. "I guess not," he said.

*

It was hopeless.

After Joanna went upstairs to bed, Ben stayed downstairs for a while, hoping that drinking more wine would make him sleepy, but he felt like he was on display, like a hamster in an aquarium. The entire countryside was pitch black, and their new home glowed like a Halloween pumpkin from the inside out.

In typical fashion, Joanna had ripped the curtains that covered a large expanse of paned glass on one side of the living room, vowing to replace them with her own. But as hers were packed away in one of the many cardboard boxes yet to be unsealed, she went to bed leaving one whole side of the downstairs part of the house completely exposed to the outside world.

This acted like a slow drip on Ben's imagination, and after a while he couldn't take being downstairs alone anymore, so he went upstairs and crawled into bed with his wife.

For almost two hours he laid there trying to fall asleep to end this difficult night, but sleep wouldn't come, and around three o'clock he got back up again, too anxious to lay there any longer.

Had he made a mistake? He could hardly believe how fast they had found and purchased this property, and he was feeling buyer's remorse. And it didn't help any that he was just weirded out by the circumstances of this first night.

Ben opened a French door that led from the bedroom onto a balcony that went around three sides of the second floor. He stepped out into the night, feeling the cool breeze, air fresh as an oxygen tent, and he immediately noticed a glow emanating from the area behind the barn. That was at the far side of the property, where Ben had found the meadow area.

He glanced over at Joanna, who was sound asleep, then he looked back at the glow, which was so pronounced that he could make out details in the tall trees on the other side of the barn.

He started to wake up his wife, but knowing she was exhausted, just as he was, he couldn't bring himself to roust her.

Ben went back out onto the balcony and looked over toward the barn and that bright glowing area, trying to muster the courage to do what he really wanted to do, which was to find out what was going on over there in that meadow.

After a couple minutes, he couldn't take it any longer. He went downstairs and found a flashlight, and then he went outside and started across the property toward the barn. As he made his way, opening and shutting gates separating one animal holding area from the next, he was mindful of warnings regarding rattlesnakes in the area, and he stepped cautiously through the high grass.

The whole way, Ben kept glancing back at the house, his eyes nervously darting all around. He didn't want to appear to be a fool, should anyone be watching, but not knowing what he was about to encounter he felt like he needed to move through the night as stealthily as possible.

Ben made it to the barn, and then he worked his way cautiously around the side, growing closer to where he could get a look at the glowing meadow. He turned off his flashlight so as to make himself less obvious in the shadows.

Once he got to the side of the barn on which the meadow was located, he crouched down low, duck-walking to the tall growth of weeds that grew up around the perimeter of the meadow.

The night was still. Ben could hear a mockingbird, which he recognized from the string of varied voicings. Only the males sing at night, so somewhere amid the mimicry, which included the sound of a ringing telephone, was a love song.

Ben crept up to the line of weeds and slowly pushed them apart, so he could see through to the other side. His imagination was running at full gallop. He fully expected to push apart the curtain of green to find a UFO sitting in the meadow, but he was disappointed.

There was nothing there at all, though somehow the entire meadow was lighted in a bluish light, as if someone had a left a television on to a channel no longer broadcasting.

Seeing nothing to be alarmed by, Ben stood up and pushed his way through the weeds, and he walked out into the meadow.

The area had been cut or grazed down more than had any of the rest of the property, but the grass was still above his ankles. He took a few steps and then realized where the glow was emanating from.

In the meadow were six large, circular stones. Each was about two or two-and-a-half feet in height, and maybe six feet across, and they were glowing like mood rings, casting a clear bluish-white light. Ben walked to the stone nearest to him, and then standing next to it he looked up at a full moon, trying to imagine that the glow was reflected moonlight.

That didn't seem to him to be what was happening.

Ben walked from one stone to the next, feeling their smooth, slightly convex tops, and their softly rounded edges, all contours that struck him as strangely feminine in form. He went from rock to rock, running his hands over them, massaging them, marveling at their soft feel, so incongruous with the primitive way they looked.

In his fascination with these strange, glowing altars, Ben completely forgot that he was scared, frightened in the night. His nervous anxiety had been replaced by the sheer amazement he felt over what he had found.

He walked to a point at the middle of the six stones, all seemingly arranged equal distance from the next, and again he looked up at the full moon.

He felt dizzy, overcome by a growing sense of disorientation.

The night sky was bright with lights, and these wonderful stones were just giving back, answering the signals sent out by the universe.

When the sun came up a few hours later, Ben was lying in the meadow, flat on his back, sleeping the sleep of the innocent, unlike any he had ever experienced before in his life.

CHAPTER 9

"Where have you been?" asked Joanna.

Ben was still in disbelief himself. "You won't believe this, but I've been sleeping out in the meadow."

"What?"

"Seriously," said Ben. "Last night – I almost woke you up – I saw this strange glow coming from the area of the meadow."

"When was this?" asked Joanna.

"It was like three o'clock this morning – dead of night," said Ben. "I could not get to sleep and I walked out onto the balcony – which is really cool, by the way. Have you been out there?"

"What did you see from the balcony?" asked a perplexed Joanna.

"This strange light…"

"What was it?"

"Well, give me a second – I'm trying to tell you," said Ben. Joanna had this way of cutting him off, in his long-windedness, forcing him to get to points he rather enjoyed drawing out. It was another reason nobody read his books. "I got a flashlight and went over there to see what was going on."

"That doesn't even sound like you," said Joanna. "Weren't you scared?"

Ben made a face like that was absurd. "I ain't afraid of nothing," he said, loosely imitating Bert Lahr, the Cowardly Lion, then he changed his mind and admitted – "No, I was scared shitless, but more than that, I was curious about what was making that light."

"So, what was it?" asked Joanna.

"It's those stones over there, they were glowing like lightbulbs," said Ben.

Joanna shook her head. "I don't know what you are talking about. What stones?"

"I didn't know they were there either," said Ben. "Over in that meadow there are six circular stones. They are of uniform size and they look a lot like stone altars, like you see in ancient ritual sites."

Joanna frowned. "Seriously?"

Ben nodded – "Serious as sin. I guess they were just reflecting the light of the full moon, but they were really bright. I mean, they lit up the trees all around the meadow – damnedest thing I've ever seen."

"And that I've ever heard of," said Joanna. "So, you go through the dark of night, which seems unlike you, to see these glowing stones, then you decided to lay down and go to sleep? You're lucky you didn't wake up with a rattler coiled up against you."

"I didn't decide anything!" said Ben. "I was looking at the moon and the next thing I knew I was waking up having fallen asleep in the meadow. Weirdest thing I've ever experienced."

"I'm serious about snakes, and ticks, too," said Joanna. "We should check you for ticks. Guita says we have to be really careful about checking ourselves every time we come in from the yard. Those things carry debilitating diseases."

"Oh, is that what Guita says?" asked Ben, which was a question Joanna would recognize as snark. She had this friend she had grown up with who had made every mistake possible in life, which to Joanna's mind meant that Guita had been illuminated through pre-conditioning and had become vested with unique wisdom and insight. To Ben, her brilliance all seemed a little rote, peppered with banalities like "diversify your holdings", which for some reason struck Joanna as brilliant. Guita was a devotee of Suzie Orman and Rachel Maddow, which zeroed her out on Ben's legitimacy scale.

Joanna would counter that nobody was legitimate to Ben's way of thinking, and so they had gone through life in this Guita suspension, lurching from left to right on her ongoing string of advice, driven by Joanna's bizarre commitment to the idea that Guita was mentor material.

"I don't know what happened out there last night, but I sure wish I knew who could tell us something about those stones, and why they glow like they do," said Ben. "I might make some calls and see if someone has some ideas about who we might talk to."

And with that, Ben went into Ben mode, going deep into his thoughts, trying to imagine a strategy for demystifying what he experienced in the meadow.

He didn't even notice when later Joanna disappeared for a time. She had not visited the meadow before, but now she was curious yellow.

CHAPTER 10

"It is probably Calcite," said the voice on the other end of the line.

Ben talked to an officer with the county about who might be able to tell him about the geological formations on his property. The county guy suggested a geology professor at the University of California-Davis and gave Ben the phone number to his office on campus. UC-Davis was only about an hour up the road, so Ben called the professor confident that he was contacting someone who would likely know about the geology common to the area of the Goat Farm.

Wally Weinrich was a PhD in geological sciences, a tenured professor who had spent most of his professional life studying the rock formations that make up the Sierra-Nevada range. He was fascinated by Ben's story.

"You typically get that kind of fluorescence in minerals that contain impurities," said Dr. Weinrich. "Geologists call those *activators*. If you have molybdenum, for instance, you can get a Calcite fluorescence in all kinds of colors. It is usually subtle, not like what you are describing. You mean the light from the rocks was so intense that it lit up the trees around? I have never heard of anything like that and would love to come out and have a look."

*

Ben made arrangements to have Dr. Weinrich come out to the Goat Farm, and the professor showed up just days after Ben and

Joanna moved in. They didn't even have their boxes unpacked yet, but Joanna had turned the downstairs bedroom into a staging area and moved all the cardboard boxes into that room for unpacking. That cleared the living area and made it possible to have a guest in, and to offer the good professor someplace where he could sit.

Weinrich arrived at the Goat Farm after dark, and after Ben and Joanna had already had dinner, a schedule that was calibrated to avoid inconveniencing the couple as much as possible. The idea was to do a stakeout, staying up through the night to see if the glowing phenomena was repeated, giving the professor an opportunity to assess what was going on there.

*

"You know, it has only been in the last hundred years that the Sierra-Nevada range has even been explored, to any great extent."

Professor Weinrich sat holding a glass tumbler filled high with Ben's favorite cabernet, his Carnivor. A large man, considerably overweight, he stretched his legs out before him as he rested his glass on his considerable belly.

"Are you folks native Californians?" Weinrich asked.

"I am," said Joanna. "Ben's a transplant – or a houseplant, I haven't decided which." She grinned mischievously and Ben shot her a discouraging look.

"Well then you'll know the history of this place," said Weinrich. "All of this through here from Nevada City down through Placer County was all ground zero for the 1849 gold rush. The whole area is part of what we call the American Cordillera, though that's a bit of misplaced nationalism because it is part of something much bigger than even our great country. It is the backbone of our side of the planet. Those mountains are contiguous with ranges stretching from Canada all the way down through Central and South America to Antarctica. And they are composed of fucking granite!" Weinrich suddenly realized that the wine was working its magic, and he immediately felt embarrassed by his word choice. "Sorry, have to mind my language."

"No problem," said Joanna, taking a sip and glancing over at Ben. "I read recently that highly intelligent people are the ones most prone to use vulgar language." And she glanced back over at Ben again. *Now let's see him tell the professor to watch his tongue.*

He didn't, of course, but rather asked a softball question. "So, why do you make a point of that, the granite thing. What else are mountains made of?"

"Oh, well, mountains are formed in a variety of ways. The lava flow of volcanoes, for instance, forms mountain ranges. The Sierra-Nevada range is what we call a 'fault-block'," said Weinrich. "You get these plates – tectonic plates, you've probably heard them called – that move beneath the surface of the earth and create incredible pressures that result in earthquakes, and they buckle into extraordinary upward thrusts, and that's what we have here. There is granite all around us. In fact, over on Highway 49 there is a huge granite quarry – you've probably seen it. It has always been a premium building material, though it can be quite radioactive. You wonder about all this interior construction, using it for countertops and such. Granite is never pure of elements like uranium and thorium, and as those decay into radon you get a radioactive gas. It can cause cancer, and no one knows it is present, because it has no color or odor."

"It's like the silent killer," observed Ben, sagely.

"Well, I think that's what they call heart disease," said Weinrich.

"Yeah, Ben, you've got your silent killers confused," chided Joanna.

"Of course, you also get your limestone outcroppings, and there you are in a whole other realm again," said Weinrich. "Granite is fascinating, because you get all these crystal formations. It is what we call a felsic intrusive igneous rock, and it has a phaneritic texture – you can see the crystals right in it with your naked eye. But it is also what we call a *massive*, meaning it is solid, having no internal structure. It's not like limestone, which is porous because it is made up of organic materials, like decayed fish and marine mollusks."

"And dinosaurs," added Joanna, with a sparkle in her eyes. The Bloody Marys were turning her into a scientist.

"And perhaps dinosaurs," said Weinrich, "though it is often in limestone where we find dinosaur tracks. Limestone deposits are obviously older and contain the remains of earlier life forms. All of these rocks have characteristics and lives, if you will, of their own. They all act different. You can compress granite and create an electrical charge, for Christ sakes! And those organic elements in limestone can glow, too, which is why I want to go out and see that meadow. It's apparently alive with something – something in the rock – and I am curious as hell to know what it is."

The three of them sat up talking and drinking, whiling the hours away, checking to the west occasionally to see if the mysterious glow had returned, and around 3 a.m., when all of them were feeling about done for the night, it happened.

CHAPTER 11

"I have never seen anything like it," said Weinrich, walking out among the formation. "These are granite and these outcroppings must have been exposed for a long time for them to have weathered in this way, milled so uniformly. It is almost as if we are looking at some sort of ritual site, these stones being almost altar-like. I wonder if we shouldn't get an archaeologist out to look at this."

"Do you know such a person?" asked Ben.

"Oh, yeah, there's a professor over at the university who I have worked with before," he said. "He has done a lot of research into places like Chaco Canyon and other of the Pueblo people sites. He knows about ancient stone builders. I'm sure he would be very interested in this."

While Ben and Weinrich were talking, Joanna moved slowly around the meadow, going from stone to stone, touching them, almost sensing as she did that she could feel them communicating something to her. The blueish-white glow coming off of the altar-like settings illuminated her features in a way that had an outstanding effect, so that as she moved around the meadow she seemed ethereal, almost like a supernatural presence, a forest energy communing with this strange, elemental beauty that was engulfing all three of them in an envelope of energy beyond their capacity to comprehend, though it could be perceived.

Ben started to not feel well. He could hear Weinrich talking, going on in a monologue way, inspired by the uniqueness of what he was seeing, but his words were becoming unclear. He looked at the professor, watching his lips move, keenly aware that the words coming out of his mouth were not matching his movements. It seemed to him that things had somehow gone out of sync, and he was having this uncomfortable feeling of detachment from his own body. It felt as if a part of him was free floating, though clearly his physical self was entirely earthbound. And at the same time, he felt heavy, which added to his growing sense of disorientation.

He looked over at Joanna and was struck by how beautiful she looked in this weird light, confidently strolling around this glowing meadow at the devil's hour as if she was in a peaceful trance, locked in some silent communication with whatever natural elements were electrifying this meadow.

There was, in fact, a subtle sense of electricity. Ben could feel the hair on his arms standing, and the same feeling tickled at his neck.

He watched Joanna as she went around to all six stones, and then she wandered off to the edge of the meadow, where the thick forest began, and there she stood staring into the trees.

Ben felt sick, dizzy, like he might throw up. His head was buzzing with an electrical charge so loud that it blocked his hearing, and then he realized that he was no longer hearing Professor Weinrich's voice.

He turned to see Weinrich lying face down on the ground, struggling to breathe.

CHAPTER 12

Ben and Joanna helped Dr. Weinrich out of the meadow, which was no easy task. The man must have weighed three hundred and fifty pounds, and he didn't feel well enough to walk back to the house under his own power. Ben found a wheelbarrow in the barn, and they loaded Weinrich unceremoniously into the device and pushed him through the dark morning like the unheralded head of this goat republic. If Weinrich felt humiliated, he didn't put up any fuss, no doubt feeling it possible that this visit to the Goat Farm was going to be the last thing he would ever see in life. And he was kind of okay with that, to the extent that at least he had gotten to see something he had never seen before: he would die having accomplished that, which was no small thing. Weinrich, after all, had spent a lifetime as a geologist, which is not exactly a calling filled with thrilling highs. These crazy stones were providing some much-needed punch.

*

"He has had a heart attack, but he is going to live," said Ben, ending his cell phone call to the hospital and reporting out to Joanna. "Christ, I feel terrible having gotten him out here just to get him killed."

Joanna rolled her eyes. "Well, you didn't," she said. "He's going to live, right?"

"It sounds like it," said Ben, "still, I feel for the guy. I guess his family is with him. He's still in the ICU."

"Well, it's good that he has a family," said Joanna, taking a puff on her cigarette and staring through the kitchen window over toward the meadow.

"He isn't so sick that he didn't send me a message about his archaeologist friend," said Ben, looking at his cell phone. "It looks like his name is Dr. Jones."

Joanna looked at him deadpan. "For real?"

"What do you mean?" asked Ben.

"The archaeologist's name is Jones? What, like Indiana Jones?" asked Joanna.

Ben shook his head. "I hadn't thought about that," he chuckled. "His name isn't Indiana, it's Tom."

Professor Jones was all too happy to visit the Goat Farm. He had gotten a call from Wally Weinrich while the professor was still in intensive care. He said he was so excited that he couldn't wait to call.

"I tell you Tom, I think this is worth your time," said Weinrich. "I don't know exactly what that is out there, but I think there is a real possibility that it has archaeological significance."

"What makes you say that, Wally?" asked Dr. Jones.

"Well, I got called because there is a couple who lives there – just moved in – who noticed that these stones are reflecting moonlight, probably, but they almost seem like they are generating an energetic glow all their own. It is the weirdest damned thing I have ever seen. I plan on looking into that, if I don't die here in the ICU, but the part that made me want to call you is that it looks to me to be a ritual site."

"Really, a ritual site?" asked Jones.

"I don't really know anything about that stuff, but just looking at the organized way that the rocks are arranged in the meadow, it looks like a setting of some kind," said Weinrich.

"Okay, you've got my interest," said Dr. Jones. "Do you see anything that would indicate who might have created this site?"

"That's another thing!" said Weinrich, his heart suddenly racing so that the machine going beep in the ICU, monitoring his vitals, started going off like nuclear reactors were melting down. An ER nurse, passing by the room, immediately came in to check on him.

Dr. Jones could hear Weinrich talking to the nurse, trying to convince her that he was okay, just excited about something. He got back on the phone. "Sorry, I think I scared the staff a little…"

"I think you scared me," countered Dr. Jones.

"It's just that these stones, they're natural!" said Weinrich. "I don't get the sense that they were somehow moved to create this space. It's more like they are natural outcroppings that have been milled in a uniform way. I don't know how that would happen outside of the hand of man being somewhere in the mix, so I'd like to have you take a look." But then he warned. "But be careful out there, there is something strange about the energy in that place. It damn near killed me, though I intend to go back."

54

CHAPTER 13

"Man, quite a road into this property," said Dr. Jones, reaching out to shake hands with Ben and Joanna. "You may need some different wheels." He grinned and motioned over toward their two cars, parked over near the Kali sculpture.

The prof was right, their vehicles were all wrong for the setting. Ben drove a Volkswagen sports coupe, and Joanna drove an even smaller Mercedes. Both sat low to the ground and it was guaranteed that neither under carriage or exhaust system would last more than a few more trips up that ridiculous road.

Dr. Jones had driven in on a Toyota Land Cruiser, which seemed about right.

"Have you met your neighbor yet?" asked Jones, smiling. "His dogs almost got me."

Ben rolled his eyes. "Oh my god, I am so sorry. I didn't even think about that. I made the mistake of dropping in on his house just before we bought this place – you know, howdy neighbor, nyuk-nyuk…"

Joanna shot him a disapproving glance – not everybody found Three Stooges impersonations acceptable for insertion into adult conversations, which she figured probably included the esteemed Dr. Jones.

Ben noticed. "Anyway, his dogs are scary as hell. Our movers had trouble with them."

"I'm not surprised," said Jones. "I was driving with the windows down and this dog almost got all the way into my car. It was like the Hound of the Baskervilles but it was…"

"A German Shepherd, yeah, I know, they're dangerous," said Ben. "Did you know that they kill more people than any other breed?"

"Yes, I do know that, I own a German Shepherd," said Dr. Jones. "He is the sweetest dog you could ever imagine, but yes, if not trained properly, they are really dangerous animals."

"Well, my neighbor may have trained them just how he wants them," said Ben. "I thought *he* was going to bite me, too."

"I am so glad you didn't get bit," said Joanna to Dr. Jones. Then, to Ben, "We have to go talk to that guy."

Ben acted like his legs suddenly turned to wet spaghetti. "Well, wait a minute, one thing at a time," he said. "Let's figure out what is going on out in the meadow first, and then I'll deal with the killer dogs."

*

Dr. Jones had a camera and an iPad with him, and the whole time he was touring the meadow he was taking notes and pictures.

"Is this where Wally had his heart attack?" asked Dr. Jones.

"Yeah," said Ben. "Right about where you are standing. In fact, I don't think it is a good idea for us to spend too much time here, because I have never been here when I didn't experience disorientation, or odd sensations. I actually feel guilty about what happened with Dr. Weinrich, because I feel like there is some kind of strange energy about this place. I should have warned him."

Dr. Jones nodded in the affirmative. "Yeah, I can feel it. It has a palpable quality that I can't quite describe but is clearly present. This is Wally's area of expertise, not mine, but it may be that there are geological influences here creating an effect of some kind, like an electrical charge. It isn't radioactivity, though, I just took some readings. None of these stones are radioactive to any large extent. I am aware of research into frequency waves and how they affect organic matter. Again, this isn't my area of study, but there may be something going on like that. I can feel a tightness in my chest, some restriction in my breathing, and it feels to me like I am feeling a pulse, or vibration. Do you feel that?"

"I feel it," said Joanna, walking back over to where the men stood.

"Oh, I definitely feel something," said Ben. "If you have seen enough for now, I would really like to leave this meadow."

*

The three left the stone meadow and walked back over toward the house, passing the animal sheds and the lagoon along the way.

"I don't believe these rock formations to be man-made, as you get with ritual sites, but rather, as Wally says, they seem to be natural outcroppings that have weathered in uniquely common ways, leaving a uniform look to the site. That is unusual, but I don't see anything about it that seems manipulated. No one has stood stones on end, or piled them upon one other, or created a structure of any kind. It just looks like nature, in its random way, has provided outcroppings of granite – it is all connected somewhere under the surface – that are more or less arranged in a hexagonal shape. Now that is surely coincidental."

"A hexagonal shape?" asked Ben, interest piqued.

"Yeah, have you not noticed that?" asked Dr. Jones. "You can see it from the satellite image of the property. Here, I made a PDF."

Dr. Jones brought up his iPad and the satellite image overlooking the Goat Farm, and sure enough the stones were visible in the meadow, though the image was not clear.

"Could it possibly mean anything?" asked Ben. "I mean, are there archaeological sites where you find hexagonal shapes?"

"Oh, yeah, it's a world of sixes," said Dr. Jones. "It was one of the earliest architectural forms, it is so elemental. You and I are made up of hexagonal shapes, in that we are carbon-based life forms. Carbon has the atomic number 6. And you see hexagonal shapes throughout nature, in crystal formations, honeycombs, lava beds. Six is what math people call a 'perfect number' because its divisors – 1, 2, and 3 – add up to 6. I'm not a math guy, but I always remember that because a 'perfect number' in math science denotes an imperfection to Christians. You know, God made man on the sixth day, a day short of the perfection of the seventh day. We human sixes are imperfect. Ironic, right?"

"But you don't see anything here that looks like stone architecture?" asked Ben. "We just have large stones that look a lot like they are arranged in a hexagon?"

"Yeah, I think that's what you've got," said Dr. Jones, then he added – "Well, I think you may also have a very large goat somewhere on your property."

"What do you mean?" asked Joanna.

"When we were in the meadow I saw a track that was enormous," said Jones. "I didn't really make much of it. I think what probably happened is a goat made a footprint in mud, the print probably filled with rainwater, and somehow the thing just ended up looking a whole lot larger than it really was. Or I hope that was the case, otherwise you have a lot of goat on your hands."

"I didn't see that track but I'll keep my eyes out for really large goats," said Ben. "I haven't actually seen a goat since I got here on the Goat Farm. It seems like you see them all over this county, everywhere you go, but here at the Goat Farm we are goat-less. Go figure." Then he had an afterthought. "I wonder if it was a cow?"

"Well, you know the difference between a cow hoof and goat hoof. A goat hoof is much smaller – except the one in your meadow – and has a wider spread, and their split hooves hook in at the ends. The hooves of cattle aren't anything like that."

"I thought you grew up on a farm?" said Joanna to Ben.

"Well I did, but we didn't have goats," said Ben. "Pigs were our small cloven-hoofed creature of choice. I never saw any goat prints."

"Do you want goats?" asked Dr. Jones, grinning, and assuming they didn't, though wondering, in that case, why they would have purchased a goat farm.

"Not me," said Ben, "they have those weird eyes."

"They aren't the cuddliest creatures, either," said Jones. "I've known of 'em to be downright mean. They'll eat anything."

"Someone told me they are good with horses," said Ben, "so if your horse gets lonely a goat is an option."

"That sounds weird," said Joanna. "Who told you that?"

"This old high school classmate of mine who raises horses," said Ben. "And goats, too, I guess, unless he just lets his horses get lonely."

Joanna shook her head and muttered – "That is so fucking weird, though I have heard that goats are perpetually horny."

Ben glanced at Dr. Jones then rolled his eyes at his wife. "Fascinating, is that what you heard? Did you know that goats have horns?"

"Maybe that's where horny goat weed comes from!"

Dr. Jones jumped the gun a little with his horny goat weed insight and immediately wished he hadn't mentioned it.

Horny goat weed is an over-the-counter folk cure for erectile dysfunction.

CHAPTER 14

Having a couple college professors out to the Goat Farm was exactly the kind of thing needed to massage Ben's ego and fire his imagination. He hadn't exactly been sold on the wisdom of buying this property, but he felt like he had little say in the matter. The money that bought the place wasn't his, but the cash purchase would have the effect of setting him free to manage his time as he liked, taking assignments when he wished, and mostly immersing himself in being Ben, the writer nobody read. He could wallow in that for hours on end, and so he had accepted a new life quite different from that which he had always had in mind. Fate played its hand and somehow Ben became the owner of a special property fascinating to scientific researchers, and that turned the Goat Farm into the place of his dreams. He had something he could write about that was all his and couldn't be anybody else's. It seemed like destiny, which it was.

There was a room off the kitchen that had just space enough for the table and chair that had been left there by the previous owner. It was sandwiched between walls, butting right up to a window that looked out toward the former marijuana growing area, where the sprinkler system was, and where a security camera seemed to still be active, with lord knows who watching. Then there was another window at his right elbow that looked out onto a dirt drive leading toward that same area. Most of the farm was not visible from that vantage point, but Ben hardly cared for he immediately started spending his days at his laptop, working on some story he wouldn't tell his wife about. He spent most of his time head down, writing.

Joanna decorated the kitchen, living room, and master bedroom to her immediate satisfaction, but she then ran out of space. Beyond the boxes still remaining to be unpacked – this was the kind of thing Ben was not helpful with – there remained furnishings and items left by the previous tenant. Joanna had personally lugged some of that out to a storage shed near the pot field – it was the first time she had seen the facility, and she made a mental note of what she might do with it – but some furniture was pushed into the downstairs bedroom for future consideration. So, they were still in a mess.

Ben hadn't even considered doing anything about the overgrown weeds all around the property, and it hit Joanna that he likely never would. He just seemed to accept things as he found them, as if it must all just be part of nature's plan, while Joanna saw a future world, in which weeds were dead and replaced by grass, fences were freshly painted, buildings were repaired and maintained, and everything was in perfect working order.

*

"Ben, what are we going to do about that camera in the grow area?"

Joanna had a bee in her bonnet, and Ben saw it right away. He was conditioned to her extreme behaviors. She would get an idea, something would start bugging her, and she wouldn't be happy until it was addressed. She would make Ben miserable in the process, because that was typically a required part of the solution. There was often something she desperately needed to have done, and Ben was often the answer, providing it didn't require skills of any kind. Joanna's needs frequently didn't.

Ben would be called upon to carry heavy objects, or to wash things Joanna couldn't reach, or just didn't want to touch.

"Do you think that camera is still operating?" asked Ben.

Joanna shook her head, upset just thinking about it. "I don't know but every time I walk into that area a red light comes on, so that camera is getting power."

"You think somebody is watching a monitor somewhere?"

"Fuck, I don't know," fussed Joanna.

"Don't say fuck," said Ben, knowing that was useless.

"Oh!" Joanna grumped in frustration. "Let's unplug it, turn it off somehow. Either that or I'll take a hammer to it and bash it right off the wall."

"I wonder how we would know if there is someone watching whatever is seen by that camera?" Ben wondered aloud.

"Trace the connection," said Joanna.

"What do you mean?" asked Ben.

"It must be connected to a monitor somewhere, doesn't it? There must be a cable."

*

Ben and Joanna charged out to the back side of the property and started investigating the security camera, which just as Joanna said had displayed a red light as they entered the grow area.

The camera was mounted high on the side of the old trailer parked there, screwed right into the aluminum caravan.

Ben circled around below it, looking up, trying to determine how it was powered, but it was not apparent to him. "It must be getting power from somewhere," said Ben. "I don't see any power connections, or any kind of a thing that looks like it holds a battery. And I don't see any cabling. I suppose it could be sending a wireless signal."

*

The power to the Goat Farm was a source of mystery.

As soon as Joanna and Ben had signed the papers turning the property over to them, Joanna had started making calls inquiring about services ranging from postal delivery to gas and electricity.

These were the types of chores that she always handled, because Ben was too absent-minded to be trusted with them.

She got the same answer from everyone she spoke with – Pacific Gas & Electric, the Post Office, and the City of Grass Valley. None of them serviced their address on Pointe Road, which as far as Joanna could tell was simply "2". Their crazy neighbor with the dogs apparently lived on 1 Pointe Road, and they lived at 2 Pointe Road, though it didn't make any difference because mail wasn't delivered there anyway.

"Where do we get our mail" she asked the lady who answered the phone at the Post Office.

"I suppose you will need to get a post office box somewhere," she was told.

Joanna had purposely failed to report this to Ben, because getting a postal box someplace would mean a drive every day or so to wherever that was going to be found, and every trip up and down their road had become an extreme adventure.

When the lady she spoke with at PG&E told her that they had no service to the Goat Farm, Joanna had been baffled. "But we have power – it's on now!" she said.

"You must be getting power from a generator somewhere on your property," surmised the PG&E representative. And this, too, was information she withheld from Ben, because Joanna knew how iffy he had been about buying the property in the first place, and she feared that if he knew the complications they had taken on, just in terms of basic services, that he might start to get a little difficult. Ben had made it clear, time and again, that he expected the move to the Sierras to simplify their lives, not make them more complicated. Joanna tried to imagine how he might react upon learning that they had to maintain a power generator.

Finally, there was the septic system. Ben and Joanna had never dealt with a septic tank before and Joanna was unclear how they were going to get started because there was not a company she called who had any history of servicing their property.

"Where is the system on your property?" one septic service representative asked.

"I have no idea," said Joanna. "How would I know?"

"You'd probably see a couple big septic tank covers there somewhere," the man told her. "It'll be someplace where a truck has access, so it's probably right around your drive, whatever you got there."

"So, would you provide service?" asked Joanna.

"Sure, probably – although I am not familiar with that area you are in and might want to confirm what you got there before making promises I can't keep – or don't want to keep," said the tank man.

"What do you mean?"

"I am just real reluctant to take on customers out in the unincorporated areas," he told her. "It can be a little like the wild west out there these days, and there are just some situations there isn't much profit in getting involved in, to be real honest."

Joanna told him she understood, but she hadn't really understood at all.

She went outside and walked around the front part of the property looking for the covers to a septic tank, but she couldn't find anything. Clearly the toilets were flushing effluence away somewhere, but exactly where it was going was unclear to her, though she imagined that she had better figure this out pretty quickly. She understood that septic tanks need to be emptied and refreshed every few years. The last thing she wanted on her new property was an over-flowing septic tank that wasn't fresh at all.

*

Joanna had been thinking about those growing beds out there since she first laid eyes on them. Neither she nor Ben had thought to investigate whether the irrigation system was working, but Joanna could envision all sorts of crops growing from those well-prepared boxes.

The house was fed by well water, which was pulled from an aquifer deep below the surface. Ben had discovered a document from fifteen years earlier, when a well company had been called out to upgrade this service that fed water to the house and farmyard. He figured it fed the grow area, too.

There was a description of the work on what appeared to be an invoice. It described a well that had been established during the California Gold Rush period in the mid-19th century. The report noted the unusual purity of the water, which was pulled from the earth from a depth of three-hundred-thirty-three feet.

Ben had chuckled at seeing that number on the invoice.

"Of course," he said to himself.

A little pump house was built over the well, out near the grow area. At one time it had been a classic water shed, with an open shaft and water rising up to various levels, depending upon the season, so that during some springs it would nearly reach the surface. There was a manual pump, plumbed to a nearby location, from which water was drawn, but there had been a time when one could lower a bucket down into the shaft and pull up a delicious round of pure hydration.

The old wooden shed had initially been constructed over the open well to prevent contamination from above. When the modernization work was done, the old well was covered and a motorized pump, powered by propane, was installed, and the old well house became the housing for the new pump. The hand pumps were removed from the kitchen and wash areas of the house and replaced with modern plumbing.

Other than the modernization, this well work was done well before the Breedloves had moved onto the property, much earlier, when the place was still in the family of Cornish miners who came to California for the gold. The adventurous entrepreneurs of the Sierra range needed men with deep mining experience, once the gold nuggets were all exhausted from the riverbeds. Heavy mining operations were mounted, and the tin miners of Cornwall, in South West England, brought the skills needed for the job.

With them they also brought rich cultural traditions and a fanciful set of myths and legends.

Cornwall was said to have been a land of giants, pixies, and faeries. The story of Jack the Giant Killer comes from Cornwall, and the Court of King Arthur was reputedly located there.

The Cornish miners brought with them tales of Knockers, spirits inhabiting the deep underground, whose knocking sounds on the walls of mines might warn miners of an impending collapse or might be nothing more than a prank.

Bucca Gwidden and Bucca Dhu had tormented them in the tin mines, the former doing helpful things, the latter doing harm. They arrived in California to dig these deep gold mines with the knowledge that down below there are things little known to folk above; things known only to those with the heart for going deep into the places where humankind isn't meant to be.

Up on the surface, dancing around the dolmans, were the Piskies. They danced and played in an endless display of mischievous, childlike joy, all orchestrated by their queen, Joan the Wad.

*

"So where is the propane tank?" Joanna asked.

That, too, had become the subject of a search. She and Ben scoured the entire farmyard looking for a large propane tank, which they could not imagine would be that hard to find, and they came up empty.

"Do they bury these things underground?" Ben asked aloud, not really expecting Joanna to provide expertise.

"I don't know," said Joanna, "but if they do it is down below where the goblins go, along with the septic tank."

Ben looked at her quizzically. "Why did you say that?"

Joanna looked at him like he was stupid. "Well, do you know where they are?"

Ben shook his head. "No, of course not, but that other thing, about the goblins. Why did you say that?"

"I was just thinking of things underground," said Joanna.

"Like Mr. Breedlove," said Ben, almost to himself.

"Mr. Breedlove?" asked Joanna.

"Yeh, it's this stupid thing the old woman said, about her husband going down below, where the goblins go."

"They took the fucking septic tank," observed Joanna. "The fucking propane tank, too."

*

"I don't see how to turn it off," said Ben, staring up at the camera. "What do you want to do?"

"Well we are not leaving that thing on, so that every time I come out here I think some creep is watching me from someplace. Let's just smash it off the wall," said Joanna.

"Fuck that!" said Ben, alarming himself a little with his own reaction. "This damn thing probably belongs to some pot grower and I don't like the idea of having someone show up on our property wondering what happened to his camera."

Ben visualized seeing someone riding in on a Harley-Davidson, seeing Tex Cobb in his mind – the cyclist from hell in *Raising Arizona*, one of he and Joanna's favorite films. "I've come for my equipment," he would say, in a threatening tone, knowing full well that his equipment was smashed, because that was the real reason he would have shown up. You'd ride through hell to get to the Goat Farm. And you'd only do it to exact revenge.

"Well what do you want to do with it?" said Joanna, a little peeved at her husband's chickenshit nature. "Can't we at least take it off the trailer, put it the shed or something?"

Ben shook his head. "I'm not touching it. It's somebody else's property."

"It's our property now!" said Joanna. "It came with the place!"

"So, where's the fuckin' monitor?" asked Ben, annoyed at his own un-disciplined language. "Have you found a monitor? I haven't found a monitor. You think Mrs. Breedlove was watching a monitor here someplace? I don't think so, which means somebody someplace else is, and they put that there, and that is their fucking camera!"

"Take it down!" implored Joanna.

"You can crawl up there and get it down if you want, but I say we just throw a cover over it and call it good."

"You want to just cover it up," said Joanna, repeating, not questioning. "That sounds like you."

Ben looked at her offended. "What's that supposed to mean?" he asked.

"I mean that you better find our fucking propane tank before we run out of power," said Joanna. "And find our fucking septic tank! And cover up that god-damned camera!"

70

CHAPTER 15

It was mid-afternoon, and Joanna was done with everything she hoped to accomplish that day. She had a long list of things for Ben to do, but he was oblivious in his little cubby-hole office, typing away like a monkey on crack. He had been in a good mood ever since the investigation into the stone meadow had begun, and she didn't want him getting cranky, which he could do when asked to do mundane tasks such as taking out the trash. It was better to just let him type until eventually the chores couldn't be put off any longer. Then his resistance would finally be rendered futile, like his other pursuits.

Having peaked in on Ben and determined that he was a lost cause, Joanna thought for a moment about what she should do with her day. They still didn't have anything other than cellular phone services, no television or internet, though they were able to use an iPhone hotspot in emergencies. None had come up, outside of Professor Weinrich's heart attack. The plan was to get satellite services, but that was new to them and they hadn't wrapped their arms around that yet. So, through those first days on the Goat Farm they were more or less disconnected from the digital-electronic world, off the grid, so to speak. The dull hum they had come to associate with modern life had disappeared, replaced by the clarifying sounds of nature. Occasionally they would hear the droning of a small plane overhead, but mostly it was the sound of birds, and the voices in the gentle breeze, calling.

Joanna heard them.

The sounds landed on her ears imperceptibly, and yet in her mind she was aware of their siren call. It was accompanied by a soothing, warm breeze, caressing and leading.

It first led her out onto the front porch.

It was a beautiful day. The sky was blue, with only patches of puffy white clouds, and the temperature was comfortably warm, mingling with just enough humidity to encourage the evaporation of the moisture that covered her skin like a sweet dew. It felt like her entire body was being tickled by a feather as her moist effluence turned to vapor, and it sent shivers up her spine.

She found herself walking across the yard, past the lagoon, past the sculpture of Kali, and on through the area where the goats had once been kept.

There was a fragrance in the air, the unmistakable smell of jasmine, among the most sensual of all nature's scents. It was at the heart of her favorite perfume, the one Ben had been buying for her for as long as he had known her, which was now almost impossible to find. Somehow it mingled with Joanna's chemistry to produce a potion so powerful that he couldn't have her any other way. It was Joanna's fragrance, her scent, her essence. Sweet, seductive, flirtatious, full and deep. She was moving through it as if it were a falling mist, growing more intoxicating the further she surrendered to its influence.

Then she found herself in the meadow, standing over one of the stones. She was unable to recall the steps that brought her there and had no recollection of moving through that wall of tall grass that blocked the view of the stone meadow from the rest of the property.

Joanna felt lightheaded, and she sat down on one of the stone pedestals. Her thoughts floated, not in any way alarming, but rather in one she found deeply relaxing, as if all her thoughts and inhibitions were just moving weightlessly away.

"Hello," said a voice, and suddenly Joanna came out of her dream to find that there was a man there with her.

She had every reason to feel alarmed, and yet didn't. He was a striking character, large with sharp, handsome features, a powerful physique, and long, dark wavy hair. He gave off a very distinctive vibration, and he had strangely colored eyes, almost golden, which stood out in sharp contrast to his tanned face. There was something animal about him, carnal. Even his clothing seemed to embody an earthiness, as if the fabric of his sleeveless shirt and the rough pants he wore were not made but grown onto him.

"Who are you?" asked Joanna.

"A neighbor," he said, smiling. He had large teeth, slightly yellowed. "I live nearby and come back often to see this place. I was born here. And you, what is your name?" he asked.

"Joanna," she said softly, almost like a little girl.

There was something about this strange man that attracted her to him, though he was unlike anyone she had ever seen before, exotic and rare, clearly an *other*. And yet, she felt chemistry in his presence, a kind of overwhelming magnetism. She could feel, for reasons beyond her comprehension, that she wanted to pull herself into him, to smell him, to feel his power, which she sensed was immense. He was twice her size, like a giant compared to her, and she should have been afraid, but fear is not what she felt. She felt desire toward him and she recognized it for what it was, and for some reason she didn't fight it.

From that point on, Joanna had no idea what had happened. It felt as if she went into a dream, like a princess in a fairy tale who had fallen under a spell, not placed there by a witch or evil queen, but by this forest stranger.

Who was he?

*

Joanna opened her eyes and looked at the sky. She could hear birds singing and somewhere she could hear the sound of a bleating goat, or at least she imagined that is what it must be. She hadn't heard anything like that since she had been here, on the Goat Farm, and she thought what a funny sound it was. It made her giggle.

For a moment she just laid there, relaxed and content, the beautiful warm breeze wafting over her naked form.

Joanna suddenly snapped out of her reverie and her eyes widened in realization.

She lay flat on her back, splayed across the same stone she had sat down upon to regain her senses, on which she was now presented stark naked in the bright light of day, stretched across this altar like a sacrifice.

Joanna quickly sat up and looked around. The forest stranger was nowhere to be seen, she was alone. Her clothes lay in a pile in the grass next to the altar, and she quickly stood to redress, but as she did she felt something running down the inside of her leg: semen, and lots of it.

CHAPTER 16

The cum ran thick, sticky and white down the insides of her thighs, and Joanna's immediate response was to wipe it away, to get it off her, but it was a mess. She got it all over herself, so then wiped her hands on the grass at her feet as best she could. She then started pulling her clothes back on, looking anxiously around to see if anyone was watching.

She felt alarm, panic, confusion. Had she been raped?

She didn't remember anything at all other than speaking to the strange man from the forest. Had he done something to cause her to pass out and then ravaged her?

She remembered that he said that he was a neighbor. Would he be back?

Her vagina felt swollen, enlarged, and she trembled at the rush of feelings and emotions that raged through her system, a mixture of shock and a sense that nothing that had happened could possibly have been real, and yet the evidence was undeniable. A man had come out of the forest, appearing through the trees, and he had fucked her, right there on that stone altar. She couldn't even get her mind around that, it just didn't seem possible, and yet there she was, trying to clean herself in the aftermath of a kind of an event such as she could not imagine, but had clearly happened.

She hurried across the meadow, pushing her way through the tall grass, then hurried past the barn and toward the lagoon, glancing behind her a few times to see if she was being followed.

Why would she be? What more could happen to her?

These thoughts raced through her head as she walked quickly through the paddock areas and past the lagoon and on toward the house, but as she approached she slowed her pace.

What should she tell Ben?

It suddenly hit her that maybe she didn't look so good. Had the man struck her? Was she bruised or beaten in any way? She didn't know. Walking past her parked car, she thought to get inside, to sit behind the steering wheel where she could see her face in the rear-view mirror.

She didn't feel bruised or beaten. She didn't even really feel sexually assaulted. She wasn't hurt in any apparent way, though she was aware of the feeling in her groin, where the blood had all flowed, as happened when she achieved orgasm.

The thought stopped her cold, as she was staring at herself in the car mirror.

She looked fine. She wasn't cut, bruised, or injured, or even disheveled in any way. In fact, she glowed. Her eyes were clear and bright, her complexion radiant.

"What the fuck is happening?" she asked herself.

Joanna got back out of the car, feeling now that she could face Ben without him asking difficult questions, like what happened to you?

She didn't know what happened to her. She had no fucking idea.

Inside, Ben was typing away, completely unaware of the real world around him, let alone any other.

CHAPTER 17

A day passed, and then another, and during that whole time Ben was unreachable. Joanna had no idea what he was working on, there at his laptop on his little inherited writing table, but he was totally head-down into it. She would stick her head around the corner occasionally to ask him a question about some aspect of arranging the house, but his half-answers told her he wasn't paying any attention. He came out to the kitchen every hour or so to get a drink and something to eat, and he would make some non-sensical remark about some insignificant thing, and then he would disappear back into his cubby.

The day of the incident in the stone meadow, Ben didn't stop writing until late into the night. Joanna, still without the diversion of electronic media, tried reading for a while, but she couldn't keep her mind on the words. She kept thinking about the meadow, about what happened, and about the way it was making her feel.

She just wasn't sure that it was real – in fact, had done everything she could to wash the reality of it away. She came back to the house, checked in with Ben, who hadn't even realized that she had been gone, and then she took a shower followed by a long, hot bath. In the old claw-foot tub the previous owner had left behind, she soaked to her neck, staring straight ahead, locked in thought.

From the tub she could look out through a window that offered a beautiful view of the tree line, a distant snow-covered range, and a beautiful blue sky, with those puffy white clouds that moved hypnotically through that blue space. There were birds singing, a pure natural ambience so subtle in its sonic texture that it instantly retrained one's senses, killing the recorded loop of civil noise, until one could hear the conversations of insects and grass. It was all there, just very quiet, like a whisper to a human being battered by the assault of city life. It all took grooming. Joanna was a city girl, so her breaking in would be gradual.

*

Somehow, Ben and Joanna managed to make it more than ten days on the food they had brought with them in the move, but the cupboards were starting to be bare.

Ben had the bright idea of calling the local Raley's in Grass Valley to see if they would deliver. That grocery chain was Ben's favorite, practically representing the entirety of his social life, as he did all the grocery shopping for the pair. Joanna didn't cook, hardly ate, and would not set foot in a grocery store, so that was the one chore that was all on Ben.

Back in Benicia, he had always looked forward to running out of food because it gave him an excuse to go wander around Raley's, where he knew all the staff, though some of them there hated him. He had written a letter to management about the rude treatment he had received from one particular cashier there who had just detested him on sight. He had written eloquently in praise of the grocery and its fine people and had counted up the money he had spent in the store over the past 20-plus years, which he reckoned to be about a quarter-million dollars. He suggested that while he didn't deserve any special treatment for his loyalty to the chain, he figured he had at least purchased some level of courtesy.

That stunt had worked more powerfully than he had really intended. Two different store managers called him back immediately. They apparently posted the letter on the board of the employee lunchroom at the store, and after that Ben became a marked man, treated like a VIP by those employees who weren't so fond of the rude lady to whom Ben referred, and a vampire to those who loved her. A writer, prone to over-detailing even minor characters, he had described the offensive clerk a little too accurately, leaving no doubt as to who among the staff she was. And in doing that, he had started a civil war among the denizens of his single point of contact with the human world. Everyone he worked with as a technical writer was just a disembodied voice on the phone, or an old photo on Skype, but the Raley's folk had been like family, and now half the family hated him. It was just like real life.

"Sure, we deliver. Where do you live?" said the voice on the other end of the line, the Raley's customer service representative.

"Up on Hill Point down south of Sherwood Forest," said Ben. It hit him that the description had the ring of a prank call, like there would be a follow-up punch line coming.

There was silence on the other end, possibly waiting for the rim shot. Then Ben could hear the Raley's workers talking in the background before the rep got back on the line. "I'm sorry, that is out of our delivery area. In fact, I don't even know where that is," he said.

"It's off of Lime Kiln Road," said Ben.

"Oh, out where the witches live," said the rep, chuckling. "Yeah, we don't go out that far. Not out there. Sorry."

So that was a big problem because that was the only place where Ben knew to buy groceries, and they wouldn't deliver, and that meant he was going to have to actually go to the grocery store, and that meant going by the neighbor's house and probably having to deal with those dogs.

This had been on Ben's mind ever since the movers and Tom Jones had reported their incidents with the neighbors' German Shepherds. They had been penned up when he met them, but now he wondered if they were running free, set to frenzy like those hateful Raley's employees in Benicia who had sided with that mean cashier. Those damned dogs looked as big as Dire Wolves to Ben, standing nearly as tall as either of the cars he had available to drive, neither of which would survive that road going more than five miles per hour. He wondered if starving to death might not be preferable to trying that grocery run.

"Is there anybody else you are aware of that might deliver to where we live?" asked Ben before the Raley's guy could hang up. "Maybe one of those Schwan delivery people. They have a big truck, that's what it would take to get up here."

"I have no idea where you live," said the Raley's rep, "and we don't have a Schwan truck around here, at least that I have seen, or I'd let the air out of his tires." The rep laughed. "Just kidding. Good luck finding somebody."

So, Ben was at square one, which meant he had to get into the Volkswagen sports coupe because Joanna's Mercedes was a convertible and he could see those Dire Wolves eating right through that in a heartbeat – grabbing his head, pulling it off. It was a horrible thought and Ben was scared witless as he opened the gate to let himself out of the yard, driving through and then stopping, getting out and then closing the gate again, shutting Joanna safely inside.

There she sat on the balcony, outside her bedroom, smoking and lost in thought, staring over at the lagoon, and beyond that to the meadow.

*

Ben crept down the road, the VW lurching into one rut and then into another, the steering wheel jerking this way and that as the front wheels self-negotiated the weathered terrain. "We are going to need some alignment after this," Ben muttered to himself, driving with the windows up, head down, scanning the horizon for those dogs.

He started looking for them almost as soon as he left the front porch of the house, increasingly worried that they were going to eat their way through the far forest and find the Goat Farm, and he and his wife. It was like having one of those Stephen King animals living just up the road, except there were two of them.

Ben was driving so slowly that at one point a squirrel passed him, then a deer. There were animals everywhere, but not the kind Ben was worried about. He had been down this road only a handful of times and was not at all familiar with it, so he drove along having only the haziest notion of how close he was to the neighbor's turn in, where he fully expected to encounter beasts.

It seemed like it took a half-hour, though it didn't, before he finally reached the neighbor's place. He saw the turn-in coming up, maybe a hundred yards ahead, and figured that at his present rate of speed he'd be there sometime later in the day. He instinctively strained to determine the condition of the road in front of the turn-in, planning a strategy for hitting the gas through that area to escape the expected attack.

It didn't look promising, but rather like sometime in the recent past it had rained and so the horrifying neighbor had driven a tractor or a heavy truck through the muddy roadway, then let it dry to create a series of deadly ruts: exhaust system executioners and a kill zone for his wolves.

Ben crept ahead as best he could, partly wishing he believed in God. A prayer might be helpful at this time, or a gun.

He just reached the turn-in and, just as he had wished would not happen, the dogs were upon him. They came after him like he was meat on a string, throwing themselves into the side of his car, snapping and growling. They didn't break the passenger's side window, but they rattled it lose, and it never opened again.

Ben hit the gas, even knowing the road hazard, and the VW jumped like it had been bitten, turning sideways for a moment then straightening back out, and Ben started picking up speed, driving ahead while looking backwards as one of the dogs leaped onto the back of the car, trying to get through the sloped back window, before sliding off onto the ground.

He had only just started to put a few feet of distance between him and them when Ben turned his head back to the road and immediately hit the brakes.

Something huge and hairy, that completely covered his entire field of vision for a split second before disappearing to his left, into the trees, crossed before him. He almost hit it, and the tires gripped into the gravel as the car skidded to a halt.

"What in the…"

Ben sat there in shock, for the moment completely forgetting the dogs, who were only just behind him. But then he glanced in his rear-view mirror and he could see the dogs, and they were slinking away, back toward their home, with their tales between their legs.

Ben's heart was beating like a mallet and he struggled to get his breath.

Had he just seen Bigfoot?

He wanted to turn the car around and go back and tell Joanna what had happened, but had to remind himself that he really needed to go get groceries, and what had he really seen anyway, other than a glimpse of something huge and hairy? It might have been a bear; in fact, probably was. Bears have been known to defy the laws of physics, to move with the speed of light.

Ben suggested absurd explanations like that as his way of suggesting that the world was an absurd place and shouldn't be taken seriously, a philosophical belief to which he was fully committed. He knew bears could not defy the laws of physics.

Only Sasquatch can do that.

*

He found the Raley's in Grass Valley, tucked in among a cluster of businesses, making the parking difficult. He found a space to pull into, and when he got out he went to check the front of his car. He didn't think he had hit Bigfoot, but he was sure hoping he would find hair there somewhere, or fur, or whatever Bigfoot has. Maybe he had snagged him, he thought, but he was disappointed. There was no hair there, but he was relieved to find that at least he still had air in his tires. That was a miracle after driving up that road, the one to his new home.

Wandering around this Raley's, new to him, he couldn't stop

thinking about what he had seen, or almost seen. He had temporarily stopped thinking about those German Shepherds all together, beyond the image of them slinking away with their tails between their legs.

Had they seen Bigfoot? Is that why they suddenly shied away as they had? They hadn't behaved that way when their psychotic owner had called them to him by shooting a weapon into the air. And who ever heard of that anyway?

*

Joanna was impossible to feed.

When he had first met her, he visited her apartment, over in Pacific Heights in San Francisco, and found that all she had in her refrigerator was milk, an artichoke, mayonnaise, and a chocolate bar. She didn't offer any improvements, even after Ben had moved in with her, so planning the menus, and buying the groceries, was something he had to do for either of them to survive.

The key word was *savory* – or had been ever since Joanna discovered she was a third French. The DNA results said she would probably crave that less recognized sixth taste, beyond the sweet-sour-salty-bitter-umami regulars, because that is common to Frogs. Ben called the French that, though it wasn't something he got from the people at Ancestry DNA. It was something Ben had picked up from a British friend he had known years earlier: the French were Frogs. It made no sense to Ben, therefore he loved it.

Frogs. He was married to a Frog, and so she liked things like grilled cheese, pizza, burgers, chili, mac and cheese, broccoli soup, hummus, and avocado tuna salad, much of which had to be made fresh, which was also on him. Joanna would typically starve for a few days, maybe nibbling on beef jerky or salted almonds, before begging Ben to make her something to eat.

He wandered the aisles trying to imagine what that something might be, factoring in the time commitments involved with each choice, all of which would eat into his day, and steal time from that which he would rather be doing. He liked to cook as well as the next guy, unless that guy was a "Foodie". We coin the cutest names for people, he thought to himself, especially those who come up with a socially acceptable fetish. "Furries" is in that realm, too, as it takes the edge off what is really going on there. God help us if we come up with a cute name for rapists, or serial killers, though it's inevitable. They'll be a reality series and we'll all get woke.

This is the kind of thing Ben walked around thinking on a regular basis, the result being that as a grocery shopper he usually came home with just enough of every planned meal to leave each utterly incomplete. The chili/corn/onions/salsa creation that Joanna had dreamed up often presented as something less, like a sad succotash. And he always forgot the cornbread.

CHAPTER 18

Joanna could hear Ben, back home in his little workspace, and she could tell that he was talking on the phone to his agent, Gary Hyman.

"I am writing completely differently than I ever have before. I can't explain it. Weird ideas come to mind and I've started this novel inspired by this goat farm. A couple like Joanna and I move to this remote farm, just like this, and they start having weird experiences that are somehow related to the goats that have been raised on this property, and these strange stones out in this meadow."

Joanna pulled back away from the door, Ben having never been aware of her presence, and she walked out onto the front porch, taking a seat on a glider she had positioned there. Slowly rocking forward and back, like a baby, she stared out at the farmyard, at Kali, the lagoon, and over toward the barn and the meadow.

This place was like nothing she had ever imagined for herself, and yet here she was, and it felt natural and familiar, right for who she was inside. Maybe she had not really known. Anxiety had been a feature of her personality, which she reasoned would subside if ever she could get out of the San Francisco area and back to the Sierras, where she seemed to relax. It hadn't occurred to her that what she needed was a goat farm, but then who would that occur to other than a goat farmer? Ben figured that one would need to be born to that manor, a subject he had opined upon when they first discovered the place. He had established his hope that they would refrain from getting goats in the event they were to buy the property. As he mentioned frequently, he was more of a pig man, which in true Ben form he found incredibly funny.

Ben had always been attracted to magical places. He talked all the time about genius loci and sense of place. He was acutely aware of the special energies that exist in certain places, and equally aware of those without.

He considered the latter to be energy sinkholes, negative spaces that resisted the charge of the natural environment. He hated the hand of man and had written an excruciatingly long novel based on the philosophies of a renowned landscape architect. Like most of Ben's obsessions, they were his alone, at least to the degree that no one was likely to pay good money to read his drivel.

That never seemed to bother Ben. He had no expectation of fortune and fame as a writer, but rather was just a guy who couldn't stop himself. He would become locked on an idea, be amazed that no one had ever told some particular story before, and then he would convince himself that no one but he could. Only he understood the real truth behind what was happening. Only he could feel the axis mundi of it all, the elemental force that animated some places, but not others.

Ben was of a Phenomenological mind. He had always romanticized certain places and environments, and completely believed in the importance of designing with the elementals foremost in mind. Places – authentic spaces – have spirits, or demons, and there is where the life is. Inauthentic spaces, which comprise most of what we have in cities, were voids to Ben's way of thinking, and nature abhors a void and so the useless detritus, of no value to energized spirits, attract to this nothingness like iron filings to a misplaced magnet. The high-rise office buildings, the parking structures, the public transit centers – they may look like hubs of activity, but to Ben they were all mis-channeled intentions, dead forms without purpose beyond whatever man, in his short-sighted search for immediate reward, might cobble together for now.

Virtually everything Ben had ever written was about the land-scape or the environment. And in the Goat Farm he found a place where the elementals were so alive and near at hand that you could hear them thinking, even smell their breath.

Ben was in heaven.

CHAPTER 19

Since the first night they had stayed at the Goat Farm, Joanna had been sleeping as she never had before. Her dreams were deep and absorbing, including lucid imagery and vivid interactions with strange and exotic entities.

A little boy kept coming to her in her sleep.

He was like a cherub, with round, rosy cheeks, and hair that curled around his ears and expanded like a cotton-candy halo around his child's face.

He would come to her whenever she would slip into a slumber, showing up in every dream, always bearing a wooden cup filled with milk.

She tasted it and found that it was sweet and warm, fresh from its source. It was goat milk, not at all like the cow milk that she had taken to in her youth and been addicted to her whole life. The world had turned on bovine milk, a product of a society that now questioned all the common wisdoms that Joanna and the rest of her generation had grown up believing. Now cow's milk was bad for you. Joanna had always consumed the stuff by the gallon as it calmed her nervous stomach, turning the indigestibility argument on its head for her.

"Take this," the little boy would urge, reaching out with the wooden cup.

"What is it?" she always asked, repeating this scene night after night. The scenario would change - Joanna would be wandering through a different dreamscape every night, but somehow this kid would come out of the darkness, always offering this wooden cup of white liquid.

"It's milk" said the boy.

Joanna accepted the cup and took a sip. Her eyes brightened. "It's sweet," she said. "What kind of milk is this?"

"Goat milk"," said the boy, as if they were no other kind.

Night after night this dream reoccured in various forms until eventually Joanna would drift into sleep in eager expectation of this encounter.

Her milk-bearing cherub changed little-by-little with each new dream, so subtly that Joanna didn't really notice it at first. She became fixated on the wooden cup that he would hand her, for which she would shiver with anticipation. She would run her finger around the edge of the cup, then her tongue, executing a kind of foreplay in anticipation of consuming this sweet liquid, so full of fat and proteins, potassium, iron, and vitamin A. It is said to have healing properties. Cleopatra bathed in goat's milk for its moisturizing benefits.

Amalthea nurtured the saved infant Zeus, suckling him on goat's milk in a hidden cave in Crete after his father Cronus was deceived by his mother Rhea. Cronus was given a stone to devour rather than his youngest child, and so the stage was set for the eventual overthrow of the Titans. The Olympians were destined to rule and central to their rule was goat's milk, always.

In Joanna's dream she was like one of those goddesses of the Hellenic world, for whom the milk was a nectar, an aphrodisiac, and a purifier. She would find herself naked in her dreams, in the dark forest, where unseen entities poured its rich whiteness over her back and shoulders, stomach, breasts and legs.

Each morning she would awake refreshed, a little stronger than she had been the day before.

CHAPTER 20

"You don't have any intention of working on the yard, do you?" Joanna finally said after a few days.

Ben looked up from his laptop. "What about the yard?"

"You aren't going to go out and cut the grass back or do anything with any of the weeds around the animal pens and the lagoon, are you?" she asked, knowing the answer.

Ben turned around and looked at her. "I hadn't really thought about it," he said. "It seems like we just moved in. I had been thinking we might need some gas-powered tools, because I don't think our little ninety-nine-dollar electric lawn mower is going to cut this stuff."

"You could probably use the weed wacker," said Joanna.

"Yeah, quit helping," said Ben. "How about we finish unpacking the boxes before we take on the yard?"

Joanna looked stern. "You have to help, you know. You can't just leave this all on me, this whole big property…"

"That I didn't really want," said Ben, finishing her sentence, not looking at her.

"Well, I heard you talking to Gary and you seem pretty happy to have it now, so you have to help," said Joanna. "I can't be doing everything, especially out in the yard."

"Yeah, right, the next thing I know you'll be rearranging rocks, and carrying all sorts of heavy stuff around, falling down, complaining you're hurt…"

"When do I ever do that?" asked Joanna, feigning shock.

"I don't know – whenever you do anything?" said Ben.

It was true. She was a total drama queen, turning every act and triggered emotion into an event of some kind. None of it ever lasted long, but she was a constant vortex of bull-in-a-China-shop energy, creating scenes. It was *her* show. In fact, the reason that Ben had such a burr under his saddle – he was working on his wrangler allusions, now that he had acreage – where Joanna's friend Guita was concerned, had everything to do with a slight he felt dating back to before he and Joanna were married. "It's Joanna's wedding," Guita had declared, like a sow bear defending her young. Ben had the audacity to make a suggestion regarding the wedding plan, which was simply not allowed. Guita never accepted Ben and he figured it was because she was all about Joanna, and he was not wrong. Guita the soothsayer was in love, and always had been, since she and Joanna were in high school. Ben could hardly hold that against her. Hell, he figured every creature in the forest probably wanted to fuck Joanna, even at her advanced age.

He wasn't wrong there, either.

*

A warm southern breeze began to blow, gently finding its way through the forest, hugging the ridge that ran above the back side of the farm and working its way down through the trees and into the stone meadow. There it swirled in a subtle, invisible funnel before moving on, moving with whatever spirits gave it life.

Joanna, sitting on the porch, felt the breeze softly push the hair back from the sides of her face. The scent of jasmine filled her nostrils, not there a moment ago, but blossoming suddenly like the smell of ozone around a water fall.

She got up and walked out to the deck over-looking the lagoon, where she scared a frog from a bank. It splashed water as it jumped in and hearing that sound and seeing the water jump in that way took her back to her youth, when she loved playing along streams and irrigation ditches. She loved to float paper boats down rain-washed street gutters, and to build dams of twigs and rocks, like a little beaver, diverting rain water to her specifications. Then she was commanding nature, though now it commanded her.

Joanna glanced over at the house to see if Ben was anywhere visible. He wasn't, no doubt lost in his weird thoughts in his closet on the other side.

She thought for a moment about what she should do. It was mid-afternoon, about three o'clock, still time to open some boxes, move some more stuff out to the shed. But her gaze rested over on the barn, and her thoughts were on the stone meadow.

Joanna walked back to the yard, glanced again at the house to see if she could see Ben, and then walked on past the shed through the paddock area.

*

When she reached the barn she stopped for a moment, reaching out and touching the structure, feeling the texture of the old wood, looking back at the house. She didn't feel certain of what she was doing and she froze for a few moments, sorting through thoughts that would not come clear.

She started walking around the side of the barn, to where she could see the line of tall weeds that hid the stone meadow from view, and again she stopped, lost in a rush of confusing thoughts and impulses.

A gentle gust blew back her hair, and she inhaled deeply, as if gathering strength. She closed her eyes for a moment, and when she opened them she looked into the open barn. There was a large, sliding door. Joanna couldn't recall if it had always been pulled back, and the barn left open, or if this was new.

Not really knowing why, she walked into the dark enclosure.

She had not been in here before, and she walked in slowly, cautiously, noting the ancient wood, worn smooth by the long decades of activities of the animals that had been kept here, and those who had cared for them. She walked from stall to stall, looking inside, imagining the place flush with nanny's and their kids. The bucks would all be kept elsewhere, probably over in the stalls with the paddocks; the billies, with their obsessive sexual desires. All it takes to trigger their impulses is for the light to be right. They become insatiable in the presence of a fertile female. They bare their front teeth, sniff her anus and genitals, nudge her, mount her, and if their advances fail they often pee on themselves - hardly the most refined of nature's lovers.

Joanna didn't know any of this, as she walked through the barn, moving from stall to stall as if examining the preparation of so many nurseries. She would learn. It was coming to her, little by little, seeping into her soul as she ran her hand along the wooden stalls and railings, imagining the kids.

*

Then somehow she found herself there in the stone meadow again, on the far side, closer to the forest now. She didn't remember leaving the barn or crossing through the wall of weeds to get into the meadow, or crossing it to where she now stood, next to one of the stones.

Through the trees she could see him coming, removing his clothing as he came, his cock standing out before him like a navigation device leading him straight to her.

He looked like an animal – a human animal – with his skin bronzed by the sun, his muscles rippling as he approached, his chest heaving. He had already gone into buck mode and would not be turned.

Joanna found herself removing her clothes. It was without conscious thought. She saw him coming and she was going to be ready for him, to stand her ground and take him on her own terms. She ripped off her top and removed her jeans, revealing nothing underneath. She had stopped wearing underwear since the forest stranger had fucked her the first time, so now she was bare, exposed.

He swept over her like a tsunami, sweeping her up into his arms and kissing her passionately, and she returned his passion full bore, dropping to her knees and taking his enormous phallus into her mouth.

He suddenly turned her around and bent her over the stone, his deposit dripping from her lips.

He impaled her from behind, pounding at her in a way that had her breasts scraping against the granite, riding her as if she was a farm animal.

The first time, Joanna hadn't remembered a thing, but she was vividly aware of what was happening now. He felt like a horse between her legs, pounding away at her cervix, jerking her body with each thrust in a way that made her moan in an ecstasy independent of her willingness to give that to him.

As he was pounding away at her, treating her rudely, as no man had ever done before, she looked up to see little creatures scurrying about, watching excitedly from behind the trees.

"What are they?" she asked, barely able to get the words out as he hammered away inside her.

"You know," the forest stranger told her as he continued to thrust deeply into her.

"I don't know," she countered, choking the words out, eyes wide at the world opening before her.

The forest stranger suddenly exploded into an orgasmic wale that echoed throughout the entire valley.

Ben, sitting at his little table in the house, jolted out of his fictive dream and looked up from his writing.

"What the hell was that?" he said to himself.

*

An hour later, Joanna woke up and found herself in the meadow alone, bent obscenely over the altar stone, positioned as if she was waiting to be filleted.

She could taste the forest man's cum, which again ran down her thighs like milk, his generosity far exceeding the vessel she offered for its acceptance. She pushed herself off the rock and fell back onto the ground, looking down at her nakedness. Her vagina swelled and churned like a muscle that had been activated and could not stop. Lying on the grass, looking up, she again moaned in ecstasy and again, as she did, she thought she heard goats, not just one now, but more. She could not cease her orgasm, which rippled through her body and told her that she was owned, not by herself, but by some force she could not understand.

Without bothering to look at the forest now, not really caring if she was being watched, she gathered up her clothes and pulled them back on her. She was shaking.

Her experience this time with the man from the forest had felt different from the first. She couldn't tell if he cared in some way for her, or if he was just preying on a vulnerable thing he found in the woods.

More than that, she couldn't explain her own behaviors, why she responded to him as she did. Where was her head at these days? And her heart? In all her years of marriage, she had never once cheated on Ben, had not even thought about it. In fact, her low sex drive had been an issue when they were younger, and Ben still fancied himself a stud.

She had never run into anything like this guy, who twice now had come out of the forest to ravage her. She hadn't tried to stop him, in fact had actively participated in the act.

That worried her. This felt like what she imagined sexual assault must feel like, and yet she did not feel injured, just changed. And as she walked back to the house she was already feeling a desire to return to the meadow at her first opportunity.

CHAPTER 21

Joanna's plans were interrupted by a cell phone call she received from Guita that evening. She could no longer wait, ready or not, she had to come see the place – had to get a look at this goat farm that her lifelong friend had bought on a whim, over her cautions and objections.

Waiting on the front porch the next morning, Joanna saw Guita pull up to the gate and get out of the car.

"Oh, hold on a second!" yelled Joanna. "I'll be right out."

"That's fine," said Guita, "I can get it."

Guita had become something of a battleaxe in her old age. She hadn't always been that way, but rather had at one time been a mildly attractive Lebanese girl with a nose like Danny Thomas, a flat chest, but pretty good legs. She had once had one of those figure types that appear taller than they actually are.

As she aged, she bulked up like a bandy-legged football player, quite a lot of weight balancing from up top, and she took on a physically intimidating presence to match her know-it-all nature.

"So, about that road," she said, as she brought her car to a stop in the yard, right under the shade of the Walnut tree, where neither Ben or Joanna had ever thought to park. "What a beautiful tree," she said, stepping out of her car. "You should park your cars in the shade. My god, so this is it, huh. The Goat Farm?"

Joanna turned around and looked at it little-girl-like, and then back at Guita with a big grin. "You like it?"

"You paid cash, huh?" said Guita, scanning the area, holding her mouth like she'd just developed a cold sore.

"Welcome to the Goat Farm, Guita!" yelled Ben from the house, not really caring if she heard.

"You bought a fucking goat farm!" she yelled back. "Wise choice!" And, of course, she didn't mean that because wise choices were her and Suzy Orman's thing and neither one of them would have considered buying this dump.

"Did you have any trouble finding us?" asked Joanna.

"No, I had Waze on my phone, but that road about killed my car," said Guita. "I was bouncing along thinking I am so gonna get a new car out of this deal if this fucking road kills my ride."

While Guita was complaining, being Guita, Joanna noticed that something appeared above her, hanging down from a branch of the tree. No sooner had she realized that it was a large black snake than the thing swung down at Guita, striking at her with a gaping mouth, before dropping to the ground at her feet.

Guita started jumping around like her pants were on fire and then took off across the yard, and this crazy snake went right after her. This was highly unusual snake behavior, though cotton mouths, which are black, will stay right on the attack, and that's what this one did.

Guita high-tailed it across the yard, making sounds like you might expect to hear from all three of the Stooges, which naturally caught Ben's attention. He reappeared from around the side of the house to see Guita running around the Walnut tree with this enormous black snake following her like a tubular Arnold Schwarzenegger; a sausage terminator, wriggling, advancing, and trying to bite.

"Do something!" yelled Guita.

At one point she and the snake hurried right past Joanna, who hadn't moved an inch, but rather was frozen in disbelief at the spectacle unfolding before her. The snake paid no attention to her at all, but rather just kept after Guita, who wasn't in the best of shape and was starting to tire.

"It's just you he wants, Guita!" yelled Ben, delighted. "He only wants you!"

"You fuckin' asshole!" she yelled back, now struggling to run in a spastic enough way to keep her heels away from the fangs of this deranged serpent, which was now closing on her fast, with seemingly endless energy.

Guita made a couple more laps around the tree, while Joanna crawled up onto the hood of Guita's car. The old Lebanese lady was showing extraordinary stamina, for someone her age and size, but finally she was finished. She pulled in behind the Walnut tree, positioning it between herself and the snake, which took up a position on the other side and coiled into an offensive posture.

Time and again it launched at her, as she ducked left and right, the nasty fangs of the creature just missing by an inch or less with each strike, until finally Guita lost her balance and fell back from the tree.

The snake acted immediately, moving next to her, within a few feet, arching back to strike once more, with its target now helpless before it.

Suddenly the air exploded around them, and so did the snake.

Ben stood next to the car, a twelve-gauge shotgun cradled to his shoulder, the smoke from the fired round wafting from its barrel.

Guita looked at him white as a ghost, as did Joanna. "Where in the hell did you get that?" Joanna asked.

"My dad sent it home with me the last trip back," said Ben. "It used to belong to my Grandpa." Then he added. "I'd been thinking maybe I should unpack it. Glad I did."

Joanna looked at Guita, frozen in position on the ground, a little of the former snake clinging to her blouse. The black snake was now a splatter mark with a tail, which was still moving, though there was nothing left for it to serpentine about. It was finished, its time up. It had crossed paths with the wrong gunslinger and now was history.

But the farm and forest had seen what they had seen, and a whisper could be heard on the wind

"Ben kills," it said. "Ben kills."

And none of those wind creatures had anything nice to say about Guita, either.

*

"Seriously, Joanna – you have got to get a roof inspector out here right away. You could easily be looking at six thousand dollars to repair this roof…"

"If it's even needed," interjected Ben.

"And that road!" said Guita. "Have you looked into what it is going to cost to maintain that private road? Have you met your neighbor yet? You are going to want to share those costs, though he may only want to pay for the road up to his place, in which case you've got to come up with a plan for all this trail up to your place, which is what? A half mile, at least. And if it snows up here, is that even passable? That horrible road?"

Give her credit, thought Ben, as he watched Guita rattle on. That spectacle this afternoon, with her running like a fool, being chased by that snake, might have destroyed the pluck of a lot of people, but Guita acted like the whole thing never happened. She may have been a screwball and an annoying know-it-all, but she was tough as hell. She used to tell the story about her alcoholic father hitting her so hard once that it broke her jaw. Tough as hell.

They talked through the night, and then Guita took the downstairs bedroom, still stuffed with unopened boxes and stacked with furnishings, while Ben and Joanna slept together upstairs, as usual.

In the morning they had coffee and scones that Guita brought up from the Bay Area, and after that Joanna told Guita to come with her, that she wanted to show her something.

Ben retired to his work in his little cubby.

*

Joanna and Guita walked out through the farmyard, stopping to visit the animal sheds and pens. There was a watering trough there, which Joanna had not noticed before. There wasn't any water in it. "I don't know what these things are," said Joanna, kicking at these whitish blocks lying around the pens.

"They are salt licks," said Guita, who knew everything.

In fact, getting her out to walk the property set her off on a whole string of Guita insights. She knew all about goat management, milking, the administration of petting zoos featuring goats, and grazing services. She had myriad suggestions for the cute and financially rewarding ways to exploit the assets of the farm, though she had real doubts that Joanna and Ben had given proper thought to this whole venture, which she said would be just like them.

Guita loved the lagoon but warned that it was likely a mosquito breeding ground and she offered a range of solutions for managing a feature of that kind.

She found the barn to be satisfactory and could imagine using it for stabling other peoples' horses and livestock. "If you do this right, you could probably make an income off this place, and then maybe you would have the money to do the road maintenance and fix that roof. Have you checked the septic? You've got to check the septic!"

"Wait 'til I show you this," said Joanna, motioning her toward the stone meadow.

"Are there snakes out here?" asked Guita.

"Sort of," said Joanna.

"What does that mean?" asked Guita. "I don't want another incident like yesterday. That was the weirdest fucking thing that has ever happened to me, and I have experienced some weird fucking things."

"Well, there's no black snakes back here, at least not that I've seen," said Joanna.

She pushed through the wall of weeds and showed Guita out into the stone meadow.

"Wow, what is this?" asked Guita.

"I really don't know," said Joanna. "I really don't know."

They stepped out into the meadow and started walking around, going from stone to stone. "This is beautiful," commented Guita.

"This place has a special character," said Joanna. "It is unlike any place I have ever been in."

"It has an energy, doesn't it?" observed Guita.

"You feel that?" asked Joanna. "It has a powerful energy. I've been coming out here in the afternoons, just taking it in. These stones are so soft and warm. I lay on them and fall asleep, and I have the sweetest dreams."

Guita was looking around the meadow, shaking her head. The place seemed to ripple before her eyes. "Has this place ever been investigated? These stones seem so unusual. I can see witches out here dancing around these things."

"Ben has a couple UC-Davis professors looking into it," said Joanna. "We couldn't find out anything from the previous owner. He has had a geologist and an archaeologist out to see what they had to say."

"What'd they say?"

"They are still looking into it, I think," said Joanna. "I don't think they know what it is, or why its here." She added – "But it's wonderful. Come here."

Joanna led Guita out to one of the stones that was in the direct sun. Once she got there, she started stripping off her clothes.

Guita looked at her with a suspicious, bewildered grin. "What are you doing?" she asked, with a judgmental tone.

"Come on, take your clothes off," said Joanna.

"No fucking way," said Guita, now alarmed at her friend's impulsiveness. Maybe it was this place. She felt like her head was spinning, plus Joanna was probably stoned. She usually was. Guita had given up on that crap years ago and had been much clearer in her thinking since she did. That's when she discovered Suzie Orman and Rachel Maddow. Those women are smart and listening to them you want to be sharp. Or such was Guita's calculation. Ben's view on the whole thing was that this also marked the point from which Guita stopped being fun, not that she was a barrel of laughs before she began her sterile sobriety.

"Jesus Christ, look at you!" said Guita, staring at Joanna's now naked form. "There is no fucking way I'm taking my clothes off with you looking like that. Look at you! You look like a twenty-year old, for Christ's sake. Have you been lying in the sun?"

"Yeah, quite a lot," said Joanna.

"You are golden!" marveled Guita, looking her up and down. "And your tits! Have you had a tit job? How can your tits not be sagging? That was the one thing I had over you, is that I don't have any tits, so they don't sag, but yours should be hanging down to your fucking waist by now. Fuck, you are almost as old as I am! What is with you, bitch?"

"Guita, take your clothes off and lie back on this rock," tempted Joanna. "It feels so good. And the breeze, the way it tickles as it flows across your skin. Something about the soft, warm stone below, and the warm sun above. You have got to feel this. Besides, don't you feel sleepy? It is so, I don't know, strange here in the meadow, like a dream. Lay down. Take off your clothes and lay down. Let it happen."

Guita thought about it for a minute, looking at Joanna lying there like a goddess. "Can Ben or anyone else see us?"

"No," said Joanna. "Ben never comes out here. He's writing his stupid book, or his stupid something. He is always writing some stupid something."

With great reservation, Guita slowly undressed, checking constantly to see if they could be observed, not at all encouraged by Joanna's reclining bronze figure. Poor Guita, built like a top-heavy pear on dowel legs, plopped herself down by Joanna and laid back on the stone. Lying next to Joanna, her belly looked like a boil atop that stone next to a particularly savory bacon.

It did feel good. The stone was wonderfully warm beneath her, and the sun was warm above, and the air was soft and tickling, just as Joanna said it would be.

The insecurity dissipated. Guita knew that Joanna would never think of her as anything other than the girl she had known her whole life, the person she trusted, who she could go to for guidance. It wouldn't occur to Joanna to judge her for the mature physical form she had become. They aren't all that way, Guita always noted. Joanna doesn't have a judgmental bone in her body.

"I have something I want to tell you," said Joanna, lying relaxed with her eyes closed. "I have discovered that I like the taste of cum."

Somehow that didn't land at all hard on Guita's ears. The meadow had done its thing, and she was in another place in her mind.

CHAPTER 22

"Holy shit! Did you hear that! A couple families living not far from here, in separate, uncorroborated reports, claim to have seen a family of Sasquatch moving through an orchard. They said the largest, probably the male, was carrying a pig over his shoulder. This only happened yesterday, real close to here."

He greeted Joanna and Guita with the news when they returned from their walk. It seemed like they had been gone a long time, though in his excitement he had lost track of the clock.

Ben had used the hot spot on his phone to bring up a brief internet connection and catch up on the news. And in a world on the brink of nuclear disaster and Armageddon, he focused on a story he found on Bigfoot.

"I am thinking about taking my camera, and maybe a little protection, and walking out into those woods."

"I wouldn't do that," said Joanna.

"Why, you believe in Bigfoot now?"

"No, but I believe in bears. What are you going to do if you run into a bear?"

"I don't know, bear repellent. I bought some, just in case."

"And you out there alone, what if something happens to you?"

*

Guita stayed one more day, sitting up with Ben and Joanna and nursing them through another night without electronic distraction. They were getting incredibly good at it, slowly adjusting their inner clocks to a natural cycle. It was May when they moved to the Goat Farm, so the days were long, the sun coming up by six a.m., and staying up until after eight. They had fallen back into too-long neglected reading habits, which kept them occupied until late evening. Joanna would soak in the claw foot tub and Ben would cook.

Nothing had happened with Guita in the meadow, and Joanna wondered what it meant. She had half-hoped that the experiences that she was having in the presence of those altar stones would also happen for Guita, who could then confirm for her that it was all real, and really happening. Besides, Guita hadn't had sex in years, at least that Joanna was aware of, and she relished the thought of gifting her lifelong friend.

Joanna thought maybe Guita would discover those aspects of her personality that Joanna was finding out about herself.

Unfortunately, that didn't happen and Guita left the Goat Farm unchanged.

CHAPTER 23

Cooter Riley hadn't been able to take his eyes off that monitor since he had put the security camera in up at old lady Breedlove's place. It was supposed to keep their crop free from bandits, but the things he had seen on that old woman's property made him wish thieves were the issue.

The old woman was having trouble making ends meet and she knew Cooter was a pot grower and she asked him to go into business with her. She said she had the perfect place, that they would get crops out of there bigger than any he had ever imagined. And she was not wrong.

She didn't know anything about growing marijuana, or much of anything else, as far as Cooter could tell. How she had managed to keep that goat farm alive, all by herself for all those years, was a mystery to him. She was just a tiny thing, hardly up to the task of carrying feed sacks, and shoveling stalls. That was the kind of man-work Cooter didn't even like to do, which is why he started growing pot. He couldn't imagine what had kept old lady Breedlove afloat all these years.

Cooter had known her husband, though he disappeared shortly after Mrs. Breedlove and he moved into the old place. The old man had seemed like a spooky character, a haunted being, and Cooter began to imagine he knew why after he went into business with his wife.

Cooter designed the irrigation system and the planters, which were hidden at the back side of the Breedlove property behind a tall wooden fence. The forest bordered the back side, so the plot was hidden away, and it was a good thing that it was. True to her promise, there was something about that grow area that produced plants larger than any he had ever seen. He topped all of the plants, yet each grew nearly ten feet tall, yielding tight buds that he collected in bushel baskets.

He and Mrs. Breedlove made a killing on their first crop. Dealing with the volume the plot produced was overwhelming to Cooter, who had his own plot on his own farm, which hardly seemed worth continuing after he compared his plot's output to that of Breedlove's. He found himself having to spend so much time at the Goat Farm that he began making use of an old house trailer that served to further shield the growing area from prying eyes. Cooter would duck into the trailer to get out of the hot sun, after checking the irrigation system, making adjustments, trimming plants, and managing the enormity of them. He had not imagined plants so large, so he found himself constantly devising ways to tie them back to control their spreading into neighboring plants. He spent hours trying to ensure that each plant got an equal exposure to the sun, and he treated each like special children.

He had next to no contact with Mrs. Breedlove, even while spending hours each day on her property, tending their shared crop. He would see her tending the goats, which were everywhere, taking particular note of the way she tossed hay into the stalls, and did all the heavy labor that he could not imagine a woman her size and age could do. She never came to the grow area and rarely spoke to him at all.

Cooter didn't know what to make of the old woman, nor the extraordinary crops they were producing, and that wasn't the only thing he had questions about.

He kept finding bizarre drawings of goats, and goat-like creatures, each time he would duck into the old trailer for shade. He had put ice and beer in the freezer section of the old unit's defunct refrigerator, and while none of that was ever touched, there was always visual evidence that someone had been there; someone with a fine hand and an extraordinarily detailed knowledge of goat anatomy.

In fact, the drawings bothered Cooter. Not only did he not know who was leaving them, it gave him the creeps that he was sharing space with some artistic savant who seemed to come around when he knew Cooter was gone. Or did he? Cooter began to get spooky about the whole thing, soon coming to feel that what had been an exotic side venture, a grower's fantasy experience, was beginning to feel strange, even uncomfortable.

Cooter determined that he wanted to spend less time at the Goat Farm, so he talked Mrs. Breedlove into letting him install a security camera so he could monitor their grow area from his home. He had the same system set up for his grow area, all of which was tied into his home security system. He had the equivalent of a network operations center set up in one of the rooms of his house, where multiple monitors gave him a constant feed of images from various locations around his property, and from the grow area up at the Goat Farm.

Putting that security camera in up at old lady Breedlove's turned out to be the worst mistake Cooter ever made. What he saw on that camera left him shaken, doubting his sanity and his grip on reality.

He stopped feeding his dogs.

It was part of a complete change that came over him, all because of what he saw on that monitor. It made him want to harden his world, to make it all mean, because Cooter, who was not normally afraid of anything but the devil himself, was scared.

He sent a note to Mrs. Breedlove telling her that he wanted to suspend their business arrangement, further volunteering that she could have the crop that was in the soil at the time of his writing. He never went back to that property again, but he couldn't stop watching those monitors, and most especially the one that kept streaming a constant series of images from the Breedlove place. Strange images. Other worldly.

Cooter had become convinced that he couldn't take his eyes off those screens for a moment, because whatever was going on over there at the Goat Farm was near and it felt to him like he was in danger.

When Ben and Joanna threw that canvas cover over his lens, shutting off his sense of what was happening just on the other side of that ridge, he grew increasingly paranoid.

How would he know if they were coming for him? Only the sound of his dogs would give him some warning before the devil had him.

CHAPTER 24

"Nothing's going to happen. Besides, what if I saw a Sasquatch, like I might have glimpsed the other day? How cool would that be? You want to come along?"

"No," said Joanna.

"Chicken?"

"Not really."

Ben got up the next morning and wrote for a while, then about noon he announced that he was going to walk off into the forest to explore more of their ten acres of property, all of which connected to the area known as Sherwood Forest. Ninety percent of Ben and Joanna's new property was darkly wooded and Ben was hoping, with all his heart, that somewhere on his plot there was an eight-hundred pound primate, standing over eight feet tall on two enormous feet, just waiting to make his acquaintance.

"When do you expect to be back?" asked Joanna. "I want to know when I should call emergency services."

"I would think I would be back by three," said Ben.

"Do you have water and your phone?"

"Yep," said Ben.

"And your bear repellent?"

Ben thought for a moment. "Oh, thanks for reminding me. I almost forgot. I wonder how you use that stuff."

"You might want to read the directions before you get to the tree line," said Joanna. "I understand that's where most attacks occur."

"Really?" asked Ben, alarmed.

"No," said Joanna, like he was an idiot. "Just promise me that you'll take a moment to read the directions before you don't have time to."

"Like when the bear is eating me?" asked Ben.

"Exactly," said Joanna.

*

Ben stepped carefully through the forest, cautiously looking around and marveling at the beauty.

Here before him were trees growing so thick as to make every-thing around him visually impenetrable, a wall of bark and reaching branches, and mosses and lichens glowing rich and green, and ferns that seemed to reach out from a primordial past. There was a thin, blue haze that hovered a couple feet above the forest floor, like a smoky life form, a lingering reminder of some eternal, smoldering fire that contributed to the supernatural ambience of the place. The wind spirits moved high in the branches above, but down below, in the blue haze, it was calm, like a realm slightly removed from other realities. This was that other ground, the holding area, where souls recover and restore themselves before some ornery finger of windy fate snatches them up and transports them back to the human realm, and to chaos.

"This is all mine," Ben thought to himself, pridefully.

Even the thought sounded stupid. The world that stretched be-fore him was elemental in ways that staggered his perceptions and abilities to comprehend. This natural world was clearly beyond deed and title, a place that owned itself and could not be reined.

*

Ben walked back into the forest for about an hour, blazing his own trail, occasionally checking a compass that he carried to try to keep his bearings on his location. Visual references were useless. He felt no more ability to backtrack on the path he had taken from the meadow than he had to determine the position of the sun. None of it was apparent. All he had to go on was his compass, which he had found in he and Joanna's junk drawer, and which he suspected had at one time lived in a cereal box.

"Is it possible for a compass to give you bad information?" he thought to himself. "Or for a cheap compass to give you a bargain basement guess at true north?" He had no real sense of the truth of what his compass suggested but trusted that if he moved in a relatively straight line that he couldn't go too wrong. He figured that if he just consistently targeted a point on the compass that he should be able to target its opposite point on the way back and so return to roughly the point from which he came.

Like all plans of engagement, Ben's straight-line strategy fell apart immediately as he found himself circumnavigating fallen trees and rock out-croppings, and so he lost his initial navigational bearing. More than that, he lost his compass, dropping it into thick ground cover while crawling over a fallen tree. He dug around looking for it for five minutes, before giving up, surrendering it to nature.

It did not deter him from going deeper and deeper into the forest, even though he was already lost.

*

When it got to be after six o'clock, Joanna began to worry.

She had spent the day unpacking boxes and carrying the previous owner's possessions out to the shed near the irrigated growing area that she had designated for such stuff, in case the owner changed her mind and came calling for it. Most of her furnishings were crammed into the bottom-floor bedroom, with a few items still in the house, intermingled with Joanna and Ben's.

Carrying things to the shed was hard work. Joanna would unpack something of her and Ben's, and then use that emptied box to pack something belonging to the previous owner. Then she would lug that up the drive to the shed, though she had the wheelbarrow from the Wally Weinrich heart attack episode and she could have used that and saved herself some strain. That was Joanna, though. Once she dived into a chore, there was no diverting her from that which she had begun, even to make things easier on herself. It was either thinking or acting with her, one or the other.

After delivering a load to the shed, she wandered once again back over to the growing area, which she had been meaning to investigate further. She was scouting the place out as a future vegetable garden, while also thinking she could mix a few pot plants in among the tomatoes, squash, and cucumbers.

She stepped through the open gate that entered the area and immediately triggered the motion detector. A light came on, which directed her attention to that security camera mounted on the side of a dilapidated travel trailer installed there, which looked something like a miniature Air Stream.

The canvas that Ben had found to throw over the camera had fallen to the ground below it. Joanna picked it back up and hoisted it back over the camera, hiding it from view.

She then peered into the windows of the trailer, which were opaque with dirt and clouded with age. "Anybody in there?" she asked, loud enough to be heard, though certainly not expecting that anybody would be inside.

Joanna twisted the handle on the trailer door and was surprised when the door popped open. "Hello," she said. "Anybody home?"

Getting no answer, she cautiously opened the door and peered inside.

The interior was trashed, apparently ravaged by rodents, with holes eaten in a small sofa, and stuffing pulled out from inside. It smelled of mildew. There was a pile of empty beer cans, liquor bottles, and cigarette butts, and someone had drawn a bunch of pictures of goats and left them on a fold-down table. The paper was soiled, moist and deteriorating, but Joanna picked up the pages and looked through them, one-by-one. The artist was good, depicting his pencil-lead creatures in great detail, right down to their strange demonic eyes.

Then she found a drawing with an image she immediately recognized from her Tarot deck as "the Devil". He had the head of a goat and he personified seduction and surrender to material and physical pleasure. And again, the artist showed a fine hand, as well as a keen knowledge of the image of Baphomet, as depicted by magician Eliphas Levi. He had popularized the image, twisting the Christian interpretation into a symbol of personal transformation in route to achieving balance with the universe.

Joanna considered for a moment who this artist must have been, possibly living out here in these squalid conditions, creating these images only to leave them behind. She put the drawings down and moved toward the back of the tiny trailer, where a wall separated the living area from a mattress that spanned the trailer's width.

There were filthy sheets there, half off the mattress, and a ratty blanket, crumpled to one side. A nasty looking spider raced across the bedding as she approached.

The whole scene disturbed her in ways she couldn't really understand. She closed the trailer back up and went back out into the sun, walking over to the planting area to see how the soil looked. In fact, it appeared loamy, which suggested to Joanna that it had been placed there to create a good growing bed. The natural soil up in these granite hills was not conducive to growing anything other than conifers, with their wide-spreading root systems. Gardens pretty much had to be flower-box affairs, though whatever grower put this place together had expanded the concept in scale and left behind some fine dirt.

*

Ben had begun to feel like he had gone far enough, that he had lost his way so completely that he had better start back. It was just then that he thought he caught a glimpse of what he came to see.

He entered into a small clearing where he picked up a strong odor, which immediately put his senses on alert. Sasquatch are widely known to emit a strong stench, a foul odor, possibly because of the conditions they live in, or possibly they are like skunks and have a gland that produces the scent as a defense mechanism, a warning. Or, it had occurred to Ben, maybe Bigfoot just shits himself when he sees people, which seemed like as good a theory as any. It was a response he had felt moved to from time to time.

Ben stopped walking when he picked up the odor and he started scanning the trees around him, watching for movement.

It felt like the world stopped, like air stopped circulating, and all the forest grew silent, waiting, knowing something was about to happen.

Ben scanned the trees around him, watching for anything that would tell him that Sasquatch was there with him. He had heard stories that the creature was so large, and of such a natural color, that one could look right at it thinking it was a tree, part of a tree, or a tree stump. It was said to be able to move silently, to practically hoover through the forest, smoothly passing over impossible terrain as if supernaturally gifted to the task.

Then he saw it, or at least he thought he saw something.

It was not more than a glimpse of a shoulder, moving in a timed way, the creature aware of the moment, so that just as Ben looked away it slipped into deeper cover and was gone.

Ben looked just in time to see what he perceived as fur disappearing behind a tree, not making a sound.

It appeared to him to be a red-brown color, with something more like hair than pelt. It looked like it hung in long layers, with large follicles and strands, the details of which he quickly glimpsed.

Ben froze momentarily before thinking to raise his camera, pointing it in the direction of the creature, now lost from view. He took a couple snapshots and then moved toward the area where he had seen the movement.

There he found the next best thing to a photograph of the creature, which was a large footprint left in the leaf-covered dirt. He snapped a few photographs and then turned his attention to the draw into which he figured the creature had retreated.

Ben walked over to where the ground fell away into a rocky ravine, where the undergrowth was impossibly thick. It looked like there may have been a section of the growth there that was carved through a bit, as if possibly the creature had pushed its way through to escape further detection.

Ben started down into the draw, but then stopped and thought about his situation. It was getting late in the day and he needed to start planning his escape. He was totally lost and there was fear growing in his mind, a heightened sense of uncertainty about his ability to find his way back out of these trees. He was a man in the wilderness, and somewhere very near was an enormous human primate.

CHAPTER 25

After Ben walked off in the direction of the meadow and the forest, Joanna went down to sit in the sun on the redwood deck overlooking the water.

She wasn't there for long, wearing sunglasses, reclining on a lounger, when she heard voices – the voices of females.

She opened her eyes and looked at the lagoon, and in the island that floated in the middle she thought she saw something. She heard talking, giggling, not loud, but real.

Unable to see anyone from the deck, she started circumnavigating the lagoon, moving clandestinely through the tall grasses, some over eight feet, to try to find another vantage point. She finally reached a place at the back side of the lagoon where she pushed apart the high grass to peer through at the back side of the island.

There she saw three beautiful young girls wearing gowns made of material so thin that she could see through to their exquisite young forms. Each had long, curly hair falling well past their shoulders, and the three cavorted merrily, like playful animals, wrestling with each other and laughing. Each of the three had hair of a different color, one blonde, one dark brown or black, and one ginger.

As Joanna watched them, baffled by their presence and uncertain as to how to react, she began to notice odd things about them. They were young and nubile, not appearing to be more than fifteen or sixteen years old. And as the girls roll around in the grass, wrestling with one another, she occasionally caught a glimpse of flying feet, but they were dark, in a way that made her think the girls must be wearing shoes, though that hardly made sense given their nightgown-like apparel. They looked rather like black Mary Janes, which would have been an inappropriate choice, not only for the light gowns, but for the overgrown, natural terrain on which they cavorted. Then she realized that they were not shoes, but rather appeared to be dark black hooves. And as soon as Joanna realized that the girls she was watching were not human, each of them suddenly looked straight at her, and while she was distant and could not make out details, their eyes alarmed with their strange nature. They looked to her like goat eyes.

Joanna had no sooner been spotted by the girls than suddenly they disappeared down into the high grass on the island. There was a rustle and they were gone.

*

Ben's ears suddenly went on high alert, in a way that felt unlike anything he had ever felt before, like he imagined a forest creature might feel in reaction to a threatening sound. He stopped walking, silencing the competing sounds of the forest from crunching beneath his feet, leaving only those he was hearing in the distance. Dogs. Ben could hear dogs barking excitedly from somewhere back in the trees, and he immediately thought of his neighbor's vicious Alsatians.

Ben felt a shiver of panic. He had completely lost his bearings, having only his best guess about the position and angle of the sun to tell him which direction to walk in. The trees were so thick and tall that he had only a limited view of the sky and had to guess at the right path by the way sunlight was striking the tallest parts of the tree canopy. He reasoned that he should be moving to the dark side of the trees, figuring that would be roughly east, which was the direction he needed to go to return home. But he had no idea how far he may have wandered north or south of his intended path. It occurred to him that he could unknowingly find himself walking into the backside of his vicious neighbor's farm. Maybe the dogs he was hearing were there, going nuts in their steel cage, though in his heart he could tell that the growling and snapping he was hearing was coming from animals that were running free. They had their blood up, the lust of canine predators on the scent. Their attentions were focused on something, or someone, and they were in attack mode, he could hear it. And he began to look around for a tree that he might climb to protect himself if they suddenly charged him.

These were not climbing trees, at least not for a human. They were enormous, heavily barked redwoods, with no low branches, and Ben realized he was in trouble and started to run.

As best he could, he moved through the undergrowth, pulling himself over fallen timbers, stumbling over rocky terrain, moving with all possible haste in a direction away from the sounds of the dogs, which seemed to be growing closer.

Ben was not in good shape and he was quickly becoming exhausted in his efforts to move through the rough undergrowth. Several times he stepped in ways that turned his ankles, and now both were throbbing with pain, screaming with anger with each step, but he didn't dare give in to it, he had to keep moving, because the sounds of the dogs were growing increasingly louder.

His sense of vulnerability increasing, Ben came to a deep ravine, and before he realized how steep it was he lost his footing and slid down the slope, bruising his buttocks and legs on the rocky out-croppings before reaching the bottom. He arrived feet first and the velocity of his descent had the effect of popping him right into a standing position when he reached the more level bottom part of the ravine, through which ran a seasonal stream.

He looked left and right and determined that following the stream was out of the question, taking him in what he felt was the wrong direction. He resigned himself to the notion that he needed to climb back up out the ravine, to come up on the other side to continue his homeward trek to the east. That, he quickly discovered, was more easily imagined than done. The slope on the east side of the ravine was steep, and Ben couldn't get solid footholds to get him up the side of the deep recess.

In the distance, he could hear the dogs approaching, getting closer.

Ben scrambled frantically, trying to get up the steep terrain, but it was futile. He would get a few feet up the side and then slide back to the bottom again, all the while the sounds of the dogs getting louder.

He started to have visions of what would happen to him if they caught up with him there, trapped in this gorge, which they would no doubt traverse with ease, while he was vulnerable, defenseless, a human over-matched by nature, completely at its mercy.

Ben could hear the dogs breaking twigs, snapping through the underbrush, so close now that he expected them to appear on the ridge above him at any moment. He looked around for a stick, or anything he could use for protection, but found nothing. He tried to pull a large boulder out of the side of the ravine, to use as a bludgeon, but he couldn't budge it.

Then he remembered the bear repellent that he carried in the backpack he wore, and he quickly ripped the pack off and frantically opened it up looking for the spray. Ben found it and began reading the instructions, the sounds of the dogs growing closer and closer.

If a bear is charging, begin spraying when it gets within 40 feet. It will run into the fog. If a bear is coming at you along with a strong wind, you may wish to wait until it is quite close before spraying. Carry your canister in a holster on your belt or chest, with nozzle pointing away from you. Aim for the face or spray a cloud that the bear has to run through to get to you.

Ben figured out that there was a safety cap that was affixed to the cannister and had to be popped off for use. He popped the safety cap and in doing so shot himself with a brief burst of repellent, which immediately made his eyes water so that he couldn't even see his bear repellent cannister, let alone read the instructions for how to use it.

All the while, the sounds of the dogs grew closer, their snarling sounding meaner and more agitated by the second.

Ben couldn't see a thing. He aimed the bear repellent cannister in the direction he expected the dogs to be coming from, holding it out before him in a pathetic final act of self-defense, one that was certain to fail, which Ben sensed completely. His heart sank, knowing that he was doomed, that he had no chance of keeping those giant beasts off him – that he was going to die out here in these woods, a fool chasing a non-existent creature, a bit of pop mythology. He hated himself, that's what crossed his mind in that moment of surrender and despair. He hated that he had done this foolish thing and now he was going to leave Joanna here, by herself, to deal with the aftermath of having married an idiot, a corpse to be discovered in the dark trees, among the pine needles and fallen leaves, a detritus in the scheme of nature.

But just as the dogs were so close he could smell them, Ben's attentions were drawn to a movement to his left, further down the ravine. Blinded by the tears rushing from his eyes, stinging from the bear spray, he could only make out a blurry form – a human form, and it was motioning him to come his way.

Ben glanced frantically to the ridge above him, knowing the dogs would be there any moment, and then again at the figure downstream, motioning him his direction, and as best he could, Ben began to run.

He ran along the creek, down at the bottom of the ravine, splashing water as he staggered forward across the rocks, running for his life, fleeing toward the hope provided in this watery vision he had, urging him to act, to run, to come his way.

As he ran, stumbling, moving as best he could down this gorge of safe passage, he could hear the dogs behind him, but their sounds were growing fainter. And then suddenly he was out of the forest and he found himself running into the stone meadow, at the far side of the Goat Farm. Somehow, he was back home and safe.

Somehow, he had been delivered by some guiding hand in the

forest, some anonymous entity who had saved his life.

124

CHAPTER 26

"Where have you been?" asked Joanna, when Ben finally returned to the house. "I have been so worried about you!"

"I got lost," said Ben, shaking his head. "But I swear to god, I saw something."

"What did you see?" asked Joanna, a little afraid of the answer. After all, it had been a strange day. She was seeing goat girls on the island in the lagoon, and she was pretty certain that Ben was about to tell her that he had seen Bigfoot. How much insanity could they handle in a single day?"

"I don't know, Joanna, but I might have caught a glimpse of something." He grabbed his camera and started sorting through the digital snapshots he had taken, trying to find his best evidence. "I didn't get a clear picture of anything other than this footprint."

Ben was looking at the display on his camera and shaking his head. "Damnit, you can't see a thing," he muttered. "It was so clear, you could see it so well, it just didn't come out in the photograph. You can't tell how deep the impression was and I didn't have anything for perspective. Shit!"

"What is it like back in there – in the forest, I mean," said Joanna, watching her husband fidget with his camera, crest-fallen at his lack of evidence for that special thing that had happened for him.

"It's beautiful, dark and thickly wooded with really tall trees," said Ben, still sorting through images. "Damnit, none of these are any good," he said to himself.

"What is that smell?" asked Joanna, wrinkling her nose in protest.

"Oh, I sprayed myself," said Ben. "That's bear spray."

"It smells awful," said Joanna. "Why did you spray bear spray? Did you see a bear?"

"No, I was trying to protect myself from our neighbor's dogs – or somebody's dogs anyway," said Ben.

Joanna's eyes widened. "What happened?"

Ben shook it off. "Nothing, really. There were dogs out there in the forest and I was trying to get out of there, thinking they may have been those killer Alsatians the neighbor keeps. I don't know, maybe they were just a pack of wild dogs. I pulled out the bear spray to protect myself and got it all over me."

"What about the dogs?" asked Joanna.

"I never saw them," said Ben. "I heard them, and I know they got really close to where I was, down in this deep ravine, but I never saw them. In fact, this weird thing happened. There was someone out there in the forest with me."

"Right, Bigfoot," said Joanna, sarcastically.

"No, I don't know who it was," said Ben. "I got that bear stuff in my eyes and couldn't see a thing, then somebody appeared along that little stream."

"There's a stream back there?" asked Joanna.

"Oh yeah, lots of them," said Ben, "just little seasonal streams. But anyway, there was someone there who got me out of those woods before the dogs got me. I don't who it was. It was all just weird."

"What do you mean?"

"This guy motioned for me to follow him to get away from

the dogs, and then I was just back out in the meadow again and the whole event was over," said Ben. "I really have no idea how I got out of there without getting torn up by those dogs."

"Are you being serious?" asked Joanna. Sometimes with Ben it was hard to tell.

"Serious as death," said Ben.

"You are telling me that you ran into a guy in the forest who saved you from a pack of dogs?" repeated Joanna, confirming that she had heard properly.

"Yeah, that's what happened," said Ben, raising his eyebrows in a way that acknowledged how nutty it sounded.

Joanna thought about it for a second. "It sounds like you have a guardian angel."

Ben looked up at her and shook his head. "It kind of feels that way."

After hearing Ben's account of the incident in the woods, Joanna thought twice about telling him about her weird experience that day.

How do you tell a guy, who was just rescued from a horrific death by a strange figure in the woods, that there are supernatural entities inhabiting the island mysteriously floating in the middle of his lagoon?

Joanna wasn't even sure that what she had seen was real. She wasn't even sure of what to make of Ben's account of his afternoon in the trees.

CHAPTER 27

"Hi, are you Ben? My name is Bob Peters," said the voice on the phone. "I am the county editor for the Grass Valley Sentinel. I am following up on a voicemail we received about some sort of a sighting."

Ben was a little surprised to hear from the newspaper people at all, let alone so quickly on the heels of his report.

He had returned from his harrowing adventure in the woods and mulled it over all evening before finally deciding to call his report in to the newspaper using an after-hours phone number they had listed on their website.

Ben had intended to make it an anonymous report, but the recording system captured his cell phone number. Editor Peters had traced the call back to the owner of the cell phone to get the name.

"I Googled you and came up with some interesting articles. Are you a writer? I find a number of links for articles and reviews to books written by a guy with your name. Is that you?"

"Well, yes, it is. I had hoped to remain anonymous," said Ben.

"I wondered if you weren't after a little publicity," said Peters. "What are you working on these days."

"Oh, well, a novel about a goat farm," said Ben.

"Oh, interesting," said Peters. "Are you including any cloven-hoofed creatures who might leave deep tracks in the forest?"

Ben had mentioned, in his answering machine message, that he had photographed what he believed to be a Bigfoot print, along with what looked like a print left by an enormous cloven-hoofed creature.

"Maybe," said Ben, seeing where this was going and sort of wishing he hadn't mentioned the goat track. "It is not my intention to publicize a yet-to-be-completed work, but rather to report a possible Bigfoot sighting."

"Yeah, you mentioned that you photographed tracks," said Peters. "You didn't happen to make any plaster casts?"

"No, I wasn't equipped for that," said Ben. "I had a camera with me and I took some photos of the prints, but I can't make anything out of the pictures. They are too dark, and there were leaves all over the place, and somehow the photos just don't show a thing. I'm a rank amateur investigator and didn't even think to lay anything down next to the track to get perspective."

"That's too bad," said Peters. "Would you be able to show me what you saw? Do you suppose the tracks would still be there?"

"I guess we could look," said Ben.

"Do you have time now?" asked Peters. "I could run out to your place and have a look, if you have the time."

"Sure," said Ben. "I'll open the gate."

*

The newspaperman was at the Goat Farm within thirty minutes, commenting when he arrived on the ragged nature of the road up to their place. "You ever have any trouble with your neighbor's dogs?" asked Peters.

"Oh brother, don't get me started," said Ben, rolling his eyes. "Did they give you trouble?"

"They made a big ruckus when I went by. That's Cooter Riley's place."

"You know our neighbor?" asked Ben, interest piqued. He had no idea who that guy down the road was, and he was eager to learn anything about him that he could.

"I went to school with him, from K through twelve," said Peters. "His family has lived around her forever, one of the oldest in the area, I would suppose. I think they showed up in California back in the gold rush."

"He does not appear to be wealthy," said Ben, "or friendly, for that matter."

"Have you had trouble with him?" asked Peters.

"I dropped in on him when we first found this place, and he wasn't very interested in talking to me," said Ben. "He doesn't seem to like our property, for some reason."

"Interesting comment," observed Peters. "Did he say why?"

Ben shook his head. "No, he didn't say much of anything beyond 'get the fuck off my property'. Pardon my French, but that's what he said."

"Well, Cooter's had kind of a hard life," said Peters. "He married a classmate of ours right out of school and she almost immediately got killed in an accident back here in these woods."

"You're kidding me," said Ben. "What happened?"

"It appears that she just fell while out hiking, and hit her head on a rock," said Peters. "It was days before anyone found her. Cooter didn't know to look for her, had no idea where she'd gone. I think he thought she had run off with another guy because she was sort of known to be a little wild. Anyway, it wasn't anything like that, apparently. The poor thing died out there in the trees. It was a grim scene. Animals got to her dead body and poor Cooter was devastated. He was never the most outgoing guy in the world – kind of a black sheep type – and neither I nor anyone I know has talked with him in years. He's a total recluse. In response to your observation that he doesn't appear to be wealthy, I suspect Cooter's got enough cash on hand to separate himself from the rest of the world, so his family may have put some gold in their pockets all those years ago. Some of his good fortune no doubt comes from pot harvests. A lot of people up here into that. In fact, you want to be careful walking around in the woods."

"Isn't that all legal now, growing marijuana?" asked Ben. "Do people still grow pot in the woods?"

"Does the Pope shit in Rome?" asked Peters, glibly. "California has legalized marijuana, and licensed growers, but there remains a huge black market out there with suppliers shipping to other states, where pot is not legal," said Peters. "But enough about that. Let's go look at your tracks!"

*

"Okay, I give up, I'm lost."

Ben and Peters wandered around the woods behind the Goat Farm for nearly an hour before Ben finally conceded the obvious, which is that he had no idea how to get to that spot where he had his Bigfoot sighting.

The newspaperman had come better equipped than Ben, carrying a legitimate compass, rather than a plastic one that had come out of a cereal box, and he had a GPS tracker on his phone. Both immediately proved useless.

"I have no satellite service at all," said Peters, shaking his head while staring at his phone, "and my compass needle is just spinning in circles. Very strange."

"This is exactly what happened to me yesterday," said Ben. "There is something about this whole area – these woods, that stone meadow – that is just different from anyplace else I have ever experienced. It is disorienting."

"How in the hell are we going to get out of here?" mumbled Peters to himself, still staring at his phone.

Ben looked around. "We need to find a stream, a ravine. That's how I got out of here yesterday. Did you bring bear spray?"

"Bear spray?" asked Peters.

"Yeah, I didn't think to bring any – I used mine yesterday," said Ben. "I left it out here in the woods someplace. I dropped it trying to get away from the dogs."

"The dogs?" asked Peters. "What are you talking about?"

"I was chased by a pack of dogs…"

"I wish you would have mentioned that," said Peters, who then surprised Ben by reaching into a holster positioned in the small of his back and pulling out a snub-nosed handgun.

"You carry a gun?" asked Ben, looking at it as if the newspaper-man had a snake in his hand.

"Of course, don't you?" asked Peters, dead serious.

"No!" said Ben. "Why would I carry a gun?"

"If you are going to be wandering around these woods, you would be well advised to at least have something on you that would make a big noise," said Peters. "You didn't tell me about these dogs, but they make my point. You have to be prepared back here in these woods. This isn't Disneyland, this is Gold Country. People have been getting killed in these woods for as long as there has been people."

"*Have* been people," corrected Ben.

"Whatever, you need a gun," said Peters.

"Well thanks for the advice," said Ben.

"I'm serious," said Peters.

"I'm lost," said Ben. "What do you think we should do?"

"We find a ravine and follow the water, like you said," said Peters. "I think this area probably drains to the east, toward your property, so we find a stream and follow it."

*

Ben and his newspaper buddy began to wander through the woods, picking their way to avoid any sense of moving to higher ground, hoping to find a trickle of water that would lead them to safety.

It was tough going, the forest floor being an obstacle course of fallen trees, decaying trunks, brambles of blackberry bushes, with their long, piercing thorns, and boulders everywhere, as if at some point in the history of the place there had been a giant explosion that left large stones strewn all around. All this time later, the rocks were largely grown over with moss and ground cover and they made for difficult footing. Every step could result in an awkward fall, and everywhere there was to fall there were sharp edges, granite corners, positioned to cause pain and hurt. The forest was beautiful and extraordinarily hazardous.

The two lost searchers crept through the woods, keeping watch of everything around them, saying nothing, even knowing that noise was potentially their friend. Noise alerts predators that someone is in their territory, and most will move away. The last thing one wants to do is surprise a bear – especially a sow with cubs – or a cougar. It was best to make a clamor while winding through the trees, but just walking through the terrain was exhausting and a person can forget to expend the extra energy it takes to make noise.

Ben and Peters hiked for about twenty minutes, saying nothing, lost in their thoughts, when finally they came upon a ravine, through which ran a small, seasonal stream.

"That's what we're looking for," said the editor, hopefully.

The two started following the water, moving down grade along the rim of the ravine, where the walking was a little easier, but they had not gotten far before they came upon something strange.

As they moved along the ridge they became aware of sounds coming from an area ahead of them, along the path that they were walking. Ben glanced at the editor, who was listening intently, stopped dead in his tracks.

"What is that?" he whispered to Ben.

Also frozen in place, listening closely, Ben shook his head

It sounded like an animal in a rut, snorting, maybe tearing at the earth, breathing in an exaggerated way, as if working hard at something. And mixed with that sound was another, and that sounded not animal, but human.

In fact, it sounded like a woman in the throes of sexual passion.

Ben motioned to Peters, and the two moved forward, crouching so as not to be seen until they could peer over the rim and down into the ravine below.

They seemed conspiratorial, fully engaged in the possibility that they were about to catch a couple in the woods in flagrant delicto of proper forest etiquette. Like a couple ornery high-schoolers they stuck their heads over the side of the rim to see if they couldn't catch a couple fucking.

Down below they could see only a partial form of a large man with long, curly hair, falling past his shoulders, his naked back exposed as he thrust powerfully into some unknown partner, hidden in the vegetation, under his control, only her moans of ecstasy giving any hint that anyone was there at all.

Ben and Peters had only watched for a brief moment when suddenly the man in the ravine below seemed to sense their presence.

There was a commotion in the vegetation below and suddenly the man, and his presumed partner, were there no longer. They just seemed to disappear into the forest vegetation, growing along the bank of the little stream, and though they seemed almost chimera-like, as if they might not have actually been there at all, their sudden disappearance left a palpable ripple effect.

Ben and Peters could sense that whoever was there was suddenly gone, and they could feel their loss. It was as if the forest had been alive for a moment, and now suddenly had reverted to normal reality, passive and subtle.

Without saying a word, the two men left their hiding spot on the ridge above the ravine and moved down the slope to where they had seen the forest man, now gone.

"They were here, weren't they?" asked Ben, scouting around the area where he thought he had seen them.

"Look at this," said Peters, looking closely at the ground.

There, in the soft dirt along the side of the stream, was a hoof print.

"That is a goat print," said Peters. "And it is big."

Ben looked at him, reconstructing the scene in his mind. "That was not a goat we were looking at," he said, stating the obvious.

"Weird," said Peters, mostly to himself. "What the hell is going on here?"

"You don't think that guy left that print?" said Ben, hoping he was right.

"I don't know where the track came from," said Peters, pulling out his camera and snapping a photograph of the print in the stream bank. "Nor do I know where that guy went to."

"Or his girlfriend, for that matter," said Ben. "Did you see anything other than the guy?"

Peters shook his head. "I only heard sounds that told me that someone else was with him, and she sounded like she was enjoying herself."

"Or enjoying something, anyway," said Ben, shaking his head in lack of understanding.

As they were standing there, scratching their heads in trying to comprehend what they had experienced, Ben saw someone in the woods.

There, perhaps a hundred yards away, he saw the form of an old woman walking among the trees.

Peters saw that Ben was staring off into the distance and he turned to see what he must have been looking at, and then he saw her, too.

It was an old woman with long, gray hair, that reached past her shoulders.

"Is that Mrs. Breedlove?" asked Ben, not really expecting Peters to have an answer.

The woman did not notice them, but rather walked on into the forest, disappearing among the trees.

Peters looked at Ben. "Who is Mrs. Breedlove?"

"She is the lady we bought the property from," said Ben. "What would she be doing out here?" Again, he asked a question he did not expect his editor friend to have an answer to. "I wonder if she needs help."

Ben took off in the direction of the lady he had seen in the forest, and Peters followed reluctantly behind. The direction they headed seemed to him to be taking them deeper into the woods, not down the grade they had been headed, which he had hoped would lead them out of the trees.

For twenty minutes they walked through woods, trying to find the path the old woman seemed to have taken, but they never saw her again. Then, to their complete surprise, they found themselves walking out of the woods and into the stone meadow. Somehow, they were back at the Goat Farm.

CHAPTER 28

Cooter rarely left his monitors unattended. The light from their screens, coupled with the flickering blue glow of the television, which he always left on, were the only lights in his living room.

They fed his paranoia, acting as a steady electrical current feeding directly into the fear response region of his brain. It had gone on for years, since he first put his own plot in, back before marijuana growing was something a person could be licensed to do. Cooter had neither the education to run a legitimate business, nor the incentive. He had a perfectly anonymous relationship with a black-market distributor who would send a couple Mexicans to his farm when it came time to harvest. They would leave behind a stripped plot and a sack full of currency. All Cooter had to do was tend the plants to get them ready for that exchange. He could legitimately say that he had no idea who he sold his buds to, it was just a distributor who could move all the product he could give him.

It was that insatiable desire for more product that had gotten Cooter involved with Lita Breedlove, and ultimately her who had him enslaved to his monitors.

He had set up security cameras on his own grow area, which was set back into the woods at some distance from his house. He would have no way of knowing if intruders were out there ripping him off, so he set up security cameras and monitors, and he got his two dogs. Their barking and snarling was enough to keep people away and they were tuned into the area they were there to defend. Cooter had set up microphones in the grow area and in the cage where he kept his dogs penned. They would respond to sounds coming from the forest, and their vicious sounds would echo through the woods, unnerving anyone who happened to be there, not that anyone was supposed to be.

Cooter didn't rig the Goat Farm for sound, but he had set up a single security camera to watch over the Breedlove plot, and that had turned out to be like opening a portal to another dimension.

He would visit the plot each day, seeing that the irrigation system was working properly and tending the plants. It seemed to him that the Goat Farm had fewer goats each time he visited, though he didn't pay much attention to that part of the farm. He would finish up at Mrs. Breedlove's, then work his own plot, and then in the evenings settle in front of his television and his monitors.

Cooter was surprised by the images coming from his own grow area. He saw deer, coyote, and on a couple occasions a black bear and a cougar. Racoons and skunks would wander through, sniffing around for potential food sources, and all of these forest creatures, if they made any noise at all, would startle at the sound of his dogs, invisible yet omnipresent.

He didn't see any of those creatures in the video feed that he got from the Breedlove property, though he wished otherwise.

Instead, what he saw was Lita Breedlove, who he figured to be around 80 years old when they went into business together, wandering around her plot naked. Hardly more than a bag of bones with long, white hair, she would show up on his monitor, wandering through the viewing area like an escapee from a mental facility, apparently still sedated from the last round of medications.

He could never tell if she realized that she was being watched. She seemed to move without purpose, never looking at the security camera, coming into view like a zombie walking through the night, and then disappearing into the darkness. He rarely saw her during the day when he was at the Goat Farm tending their plants. When he did she was usually sitting on that deck by the lagoon, staring at the floating island.

Her televised nocturnal walks made Cooter uncomfortable, and things got progressively stranger. Some nights he would catch images of Mrs. Breedlove, and Cooter would have to squint to make out the black and white image, but it looked to him like she was streaked and splattered with some dark substance, like oil. Or blood. And some nights she would be carrying an axe.

If that wasn't unnerving enough, there were also the drawings. Someone was leaving drawings – strange drawings – in the trailer that Mrs. Breedlove had parked near her plot. Cooter would show up and someone would have been there and drawn these pictures of weird goat people, which they had apparently left there for him to find.

He had gone through phases in his response to these strange art objects. At first it mystified him. He couldn't imagine that Mrs. Breedlove drew these things. And then it unnerved him to think that someone was there, aware of his presence and leaving little messages that he was not alone. Then the drawings themselves started to get to him.

They were just weird and weirdly detailed, accentuating depictions of anatomical parts in ways that were graphic and obscene. The goat people were part male, part female, and they triggered every neurotic impulse in Cooter's makeup. He couldn't tell if he was looking at the work of a talented prankster or a madman, but either way it freaked him out to arrive each day to find a new set of these sketches, apparently left for him to discover.

Then they started showing up on his monitor.

Cooter was sitting at his desk one evening when he noticed motion on the Breedlove monitor, as if something was moving in front of the camera lens, partially blocking the view, and then suddenly the full image of one of those goat drawings filled the screen of the monitor. It was there for a second, a shaky imagine being held up before the camera lens, and then it was gone and he could see the plot again unobstructed, until Lita Breedlove wandered by at the far range of the camera.

Someone was there creating more of those strange images, and Mrs. Breedlove – did she even know that someone else was there? Cooter couldn't tell, he could only stare at that monitor, stunned and shaken by what he was seeing.

Then he saw something that startled him so that he leaped up from his chair and stepped back away from his screens.

Something huge walked before the camera. He couldn't tell what it was, but only caught a glimpse of long, curly hair, and what appeared to be horns.

CHAPTER 29

Dr. Jones, the archaeologist from UC-Davis, showed up with a team of surveyors, and they set about surveying the meadow, meticulously charting the rock outcroppings to determine their positions relative to one another.

"Okay, this is a little nutty, I know, but I think there is something unusual about this site. What we have found, speaking as an archaeologist, is that some ancient stone architectures seem to be arranged to mirror certain celestial clusters. It looks to me like these form a hexagon, but I thought it might be worth mapping the meadow and see if it somehow correlates to a constellation."

"Are you changing your mind, thinking this *has* been some sort of a ritual site?" asked Ben, excited by the prospect.

"The uniformity of these stones – their size and shape, and the way they have seemingly been milled to a certain specification – all makes me wonder. I have not seen a ritual site that had numerous altars, if that's what these stones are. That doesn't fit with my experience. We may just be fishing with wild ideas, but I have some budget to work with so I hired these surveyors for the day so we could plot this place out. I hope you don't mind."

"No, not at all," said Ben. "It will become part of my story."

The archaeologist looked at him questioningly, but Ben just waved him off. He hadn't told anyone other than his agent about what he was writing.

The surveying team got their work done quickly that afternoon, and a few days later Ben got a call from Dr. Jones.

"Ben, I have some really interesting results for you, though me and my team would need to come back out to confirm this. The rocks in the meadow do not correlate to any star system that I could identify, but I started thinking about something the surveyors noticed. We did not make these a part of our ground survey, but there is a ring of rocks around the outside of the meadow. They go off into the forest and we didn't really make any effort to follow them, but they seem to have a shape to them. I got to thinking about it and wondering if they are not part of the structure."

"The structure?" asks Ben.

"I think it's Saturn," said the archaeologist. "I got the survey results back and those rocks – there are six of the large ones – are organized in a perfect hexagonal arrangement. You know what does that? Saturn. There is something weird going on with the energy on that planet, and I'm no astrophysicist but studies of energy coming from there indicate some kind of hexagonal form. And then I thought of those smaller stones around the outside of the meadow, and I began to wonder if those could possibly correlate to the rings of Saturn."

"You got to be kidding," said Ben.

"I may be wrong, and I'd like to find out by coming out and tracing out those stones we didn't map in the last pass. I bet a dollar to a donut that they form a circle around the meadow, like the rings around Saturn."

CHAPTER 30

Ben invited the survey team back out to the property, but he couldn't wait to explore the stones himself.

Ben went to the meadow early the next morning, while Joanna was still in bed asleep, and he located the line of rocks he had been told about. He started following the line, which quickly led him into the forest.

There were stones there, covered in moss and pine needles and not always visible, but Ben walked along uncovering them until he could look back and see that they were clearly visible, and obviously arranged in a giant circle around the stone meadow.

He then made an interesting discovery.

Following the circle of rocks out of the forest and back into the farm yard, he realized that most were covered by long grass, but that their path cut right through the heart of the lagoon, where the floating island was. He then found rocks continuing from the lagoon, running along the edge of the deck that had been built there, and then continuing across the property until they entered back into the forest to complete the circle at the back side of the meadow. Ben had seen this row of rocks in the yard, but as they paralleled a walkway he had assumed they were simply delineating that path.

Were they supposed to represent the rings of Saturn?

And if so, why?

*

"So. why Saturn?"

Dr. Jones returned with his survey team the next day to survey the larger site, including the stones ringing the stone meadow. He was talking about the planet Saturn from the time he got out of his car and met Ben in the yard in front of the house.

"Saturn has been influencing cultures for as long as known human civilization has existed, starting with the Sumerians," Jones told Ben. "In ancient Mesopotamia, for instance, the planet Saturn was viewed as a god they called Ninurta. Ninurta was hugely influential. He provided the knowledge of agricultural development, and of healing, but then he did this heroic thing, that put him in another league as a God. He fought this weird monster bird named Anzu, who had stolen the Tablet of Destinies. Some sources call Anzu a dragon, but he had an eagle-like head in most images."

"Ninurta was the son of Enlil, one of the creators of humankind, and Ninurta accomplished this feat that several before him had failed to do, and so he became not only a god of farming and healing, but also of war. He became a warrior, so you had this thing going on with him that was both male and female. He was a caring nurturer who could kill – and for a time he held those tablets, which were the laws of the universe. The Babylonians called Saturn 'Sagush', and Sagush – Ninurta – was the very embodiment of law and order."

Dr. Jones told this story as he and Ben crossed the Goat Farm on their way toward the stone meadow, with the survey team following along.

"Why do you think this might be relevant to our meadow?" asked Ben, not at all following Dr. Jones' train of thought.

"This is going to be hard to explain," said Jones, "but ancient people seemed to have been a lot closer to nature than we are today. Everything, even the stones and rocks, were animated with spirits, and Ninurta was said to have imposed his rule, his sense of order, on the minerals of the earth. Those elements, in the Babylonian myth, had sided with Anzu, and so to control them Ninurta – Sagush, the planet Saturn – assigned them with their natures. He imposed himself upon them."

Jones stop talking for a moment, which led Ben to imagine that he was about to finish his point, but when he said nothing, Ben pressed – "So, what has that to do with what we are doing here today."

"Call me insane but I think Ninurta is still at work," said Jones.

"What, in our meadow?" asked Ben, with a tone that screamed disbelief.

"It is a philosophical thing, but yes, in your meadow and in our world," said Jones.

"You are being serious, right?" asked Ben.

"There is a weird thing about Ninurta – or maybe not weird, but human," said Jones, as they continued toward the meadow. "Power went to his head. He was elevated to the council of the Gods as reward for returning the tablets to Enlil. In Greek mythology, Ninurta is the Titan Kronos. He created the separation between the earth and the sky, because in the Greek myth Kronos was born of a union between Gaia and Ouranos – Earth and Sky.

"The sky – the cosmos – represented law and order, while the earth represented chaos," Jones continued. "The Sky god Ouranos was preventing his wife, the Earth goddess Gaia, from giving birth to children. Kronos intervened, castrating Ouranos, which cemented this distinction between heaven and earth, or so the story goes."

"That doesn't make any sense," said Ben, listening closely. "It sounds like Ouranos liked the sex but not the kids, who were disorderly."

"That's what it sounds like to me, too," said Jones. "Kronos opened the door to the chaos of earthly humanity, even while his nature is to impose law and order."

"He is confused," summed Ben.

"Or fully realized, depending upon your point of view," said

Jones. "He is dualism, balance, the perfect blend of yin and yang, if you'll allow me to mix my philosophical references."

"And this has what to do with my meadow?" asked Ben, as the two arrived at the site.

"I am exploring the possibility that your meadow, like other ancient sites aligned to celestial bodies, is some kind of a receiver for messages coming from outside of our human realm," said Jones.

"That's fucking nuts," said Ben.

"Yep, totally insane," agreed Jones, "but you seem to have something outside of the normal happening here on your property. I might even call it supernatural. I am just looking at the possible reasons for that, and this is the best I've come up with."

*

Ben spent the afternoon watching the surveyors set up their equipment and then move from position to position as they took measurements on the area, concentrating on the concentric ring of stones that put the six altar stones in the stone meadow at their center.

One-by-one, the surveyors fell to the influence of the meadow, becoming disoriented and having to retreat to the barn to recover. Over the course of the afternoon, the building became a triage center, a place where the team could rehydrate and pull themselves back together before going at it again, returning to their duties, surveying the exact locations of the stone perimeter that had been so carefully arranged.

Two days later, Ben got a call from Dr. Tom Jones.

"It is a perfect match," he told Ben. "What you have there in the meadow, and in those stones surrounding that meadow, is an earthly representation of not only the planet Saturn, but with whatever is going on with that planet that is creating that weird hexagonal energy form."

"So, what does it mean?" asked Ben.

"I really have no idea," said Dr. Jones. "It may be that my little human brain is simply not big enough to comprehend what is going on there."

CHAPTER 31

What did it mean that the rings around the stone meadow – the ring around Saturn – ran right through the lagoon, and the floating island?

The question got into Ben's head and became his obsession.

After talking with Dr. Jones, and listening to his strange celestial theory, Ben's imagination took a hold on him and the lagoon and the floating island became all he could think about. He began to imagine that the watery satellite was somehow fundamental to the organization of whatever system was at work in the stone meadow. Perhaps, like the moons of Saturn that organize the rings around that planet until they are flat and grooved like an old vinyl recording, that orb – that floating, other-dimensional droplet of inaccessible reality – held the key. His curiosity became ungovernable.

The next morning, Ben got up early, and instead of going to his writing he went to the mudroom off the kitchen and got himself equipped for what he had determined he must do.

He dawned a pair of hip waders, left behind by the previous owner, and as the sun came up, he wandered into the purple dawn and out to the edge of the lagoon. There he paused for a moment, looking around, as if there was a chance that he was other than alone, and then he cautiously waded out into the waters, moving carefully, feeling the bottom with his heavily rubberized right foot, probing one step at a time with the idea of slowly introducing himself to how deep the water was.

The property description had included no information about the size of the lagoon, which Ben estimated to be somewhere between one-hundred-fifty and one-hundred-sixty feet in diameter. The center of it, the middle third, was this island that had become the center of his intrigue.

It was impossible to tell if it remained in the middle of the lagoon because it was literally an island, or if it was a living patch of water grass that for some reason floated on top but stayed anchored in place.

The water around him was remarkably clear. He seemed to be able to see the bottom, so it didn't seem that the water was deep, which gave Ben confidence that he could walk along the bottom to reach the island.

He got only halfway when suddenly he felt the bottom fall away sharply and he suddenly disappeared beneath the surface. He quickly popped back up, but just as quickly water began to pour into his waders and what were intended to keep him dry suddenly began to weigh him down, until he could barely keep his nostrils above the water line. He fought to resurface and struggle back toward the safety of the bank, growing increasingly panicked as he realized he was going further down. He had no idea the water was so deep. He could see the bottom, which seemed so close that he could reach down and touch it, but it must not have been what he perceived. Ben found himself in fifteen feet of water, weighted down like a dog in a bag of rocks, and he had never learned to swim.

Panic gripped him as he realized that he was going to drown.

As he sunk deeper, he struggled to pull the water-filled waders off of him, but the rubber was slick and resisted his frantic tugs. Water rushed into his lungs.

He was losing and could feel it. He was going to die.

As he struggled, Ben kicked up sediment from the floor of the lagoon, and the previously clear waters began to fill with clouds until Ben was surrounded by them, engulfed by a liquid blanket, opaque with a soft brown color, and then through that wall of strange color there appeared the forms of three beautiful young women, their hair floating around him with the clouds of sediment. They rose from the bottom of the lagoon, moving up around him, pushing him up to the air, and away from death.

Ben could feel himself being transported through the water, up from the bottom to the breathing air, and then he was lying on the bank, coughing water from his lungs, struggling for life.

As the air came back into him, he lay there in an exhausted state.

Then he raised his head to look back at the water, back to the three girls in the lagoon, but they were no longer there. The waters had returned to their normal state of serene calm. The milky grace of salvation had settled, and the water was clear again.

Ben lay on the bank of the lagoon for many minutes, and then struggled to his feet and walked, as best he could, back to the house. The waders were still filled with water and he couldn't wait to get them off, but he waited until he had traversed the rocky path, so at least he didn't walk it with bare feet.

Outside the mud room, Ben stopped and pulled the galling rubber off his hips and legs, though it clung to him like a virus, oozing liquid and squeaking as Ben fought to free himself of the inhuman prophylactic. Once he had the waders off, he tossed them contemptuously away from the house, as if they were evil and he never wanted to see them again.

The clothes he wore beneath were soaking wet, and Ben stripped naked in the mud room, leaving his soggy clothes in a pile on the floor, and then he went directly to the bathroom, where he quickly showered. The lagoon water was remarkably clean and fresh, but Ben wanted it off of him, to wash it away like a bad memory of something he wished had never happened.

After he got out of the shower, he wrapped a towel around his waist and then went to he and Joanna's bedroom, where he sat himself down at the foot of their bed.

For many minutes he sat there, staring at the floor, thinking, until finally Joanna was awakened by her growing awareness of his presence. She was used to his early morning hours, accustomed to waking up alone. She had rarely awakened to find him still there, let alone to find him sitting on the bed staring into space as if in a state of shock.

"Ben?" she asked, as if she wasn't sure it was him.

Ben didn't respond, but just kept staring at the floor.

"Ben?" said Joanna, "are you okay?"

When again he did not respond, Joanna sat up in bed and moved to his side, putting her arms around him. "Ben, what's wrong?" she asked.

"I don't know," he finally said. "There is something wrong with me. It is as if I have lost my senses."

Joanna looked concerned. "What do you mean?"

"Obsessing on things, thinking crazy thoughts."

Ben seemed spacey, as if he was in a dream state and talking to himself.

"Chasing fantasies in the woods, imagining that our meadow is somehow related to a distant planet."

Joanna didn't understand what he was saying. "What are you talking about?" she asked, a little desperation in her voice. He was scaring her, like a stranger who had shown up in her bedroom, talking in cryptic ways.

"I almost got myself killed," Ben said, finally saying something Joanna could understand.

"What do you mean?" asked Joanna.

"I went out into the lagoon," said Ben.

"Into the water?" asked Joanna, shocked. She knew that Ben had an aversion to water, that he couldn't swim and so avoided water like it was plague. What would possess him to go into the lagoon?

"I was thinking about Jones, what Jones was saying," said Ben.

Joanna stared at him like he was channeling a spirit.

"I was thinking about the ring that he found around the stone meadow, and about how it intersects to the lagoon, and the island," said Ben, reporting events in a trance-like state. "I don't know what is in my head, but I couldn't stop thinking about it, and I found those waders that were left here, and I put them on and tried to walk out into the lagoon to get to the island."

Joanna's eyes widened. She thought of the strange girls she had imagined seeing on that island, cavorting among the tall grass; the goat girls, which she had convinced herself were a product of her own fevered imagination.

Ben had no idea. If he thought his mind was filled with strange thoughts and images, what if he knew about hers?

"I was drowning, Joanna," Ben said, still staring at the floor. "My lungs filled with water and I could feel that I was starting to die, and that my spirit could feel what was happening and was preparing to leave my body, to give this part of me up for dead, and to move on. But just as I knew my life was over there appeared, as if out of clouds, these beautiful young girls."

Joanna sat silently, in her own kind of shock.

The girls on the floating island were real, as real as her forest stranger. She knew that now, because Ben now recognized a reality that she thought had been only hers. Now Ben, too, was drowning in whatever it was that was going on at the Goat Farm, just as was she.

156

CHAPTER 32

"What are you doing?" asked Ben.

Joanna was a fastidious homemaker and an excellent home designer, and she enjoyed refinishing vintage furniture, and had even brought several pianos back to life. She was not, however, someone inclined to do arts and crafts, so Ben was surprised to find her in the sun room weaving together some sort of arrangement made of broad-bladed grass, straw, and other materials she had recovered from the property.

"I'm making something," she said.

"What is it?" asked Ben.

"Well, don't laugh at me, it's just an idea," said Joanna. "I know you are the creative one, but I found this behind one of the goat sheds."

She reached down beside her and pulled up an animal skull, with two long hooked antlers.

"What the hell?" shrieked Ben, his jaw dropping.

"It's a goat head," said Joanna. "I thought I could create this wall hanging, kind of like that one."

She pointed at that other skull, the red-lacquered one left by the previous occupants, that Joanna had promised to take down but never got around to. It gave Ben the creeps. It looked like it might have been a cow of some kind, though the kind was unclear to him, and that someone had painted it a garish red struck Ben as spooky.

It was a skull with the flesh pulled away.

"I thought we were going to throw that thing away," said Ben.

"I sort of like it," Joanna said.

"And so you are building another?" asked Ben. "That's just what we need."

"Well, mine's going to be pretty," said Joanna. "See all this natural stuff I have found to nest her in. I'm going to call her the Whore of Baphomet."

Ben went white. "You are kidding me! Where did you come up with that name?"

Joanna looked shocked by his reaction. "I don't know, it just came to me. I remembered that old Levi painting and the name just came to me."

"That's the name of my novel!" said Ben.

"What novel?" asked Joanna.

"The one I've been working on since we got here," said Ben. "I didn't want to tell you about it, I was going to surprise you with it. It's a horror story."

"Horror or whore?" asked Joanna.

"The scary one," said Ben.

"I'm not sure which one that is," muttered Joanna, going back to her work.

CHAPTER 33

Early the next morning, Ben was working at his laptop in his little writing room when he was surprised by a knock on the door. He looked up from his work and stared for a moment through the window, thinking. Someone had let themselves through the gate and into the yard.

Ben stood up from his table and moved cautiously to the doorway, where he could see the front porch, and there he saw two uniformed policemen.

"Hello, I am Officer Tyndall and this is Officer Yates," said the older of the two as Ben opened the front door.

The second officer doffed his hat briefly.

"Our apologies for dropping in on you like this, but we are investigating a missing persons case and wonder if we might ask you a few questions," said Officer Tyndall.

"A missing person's case?" asked Ben. "Who are you looking for?"

"A senior by the name of Lita Breedlove," said Tyndall.

"Mrs. Breedlove is missing?" asked Ben. "That's who we bought this place from. What has happened with her?"

Tyndall's expression told Ben that he wasn't sure. "She passed out on the street in Grass Valley a couple days ago and was taken to the ER over at Sierra-Nevada Memorial. She seems to have disappeared from there."

"Disappeared?" asked Ben.

"She was left unattended for a time and apparently left the hospital unnoticed," said the officer. "No one has any idea where she has gone. The staff there doesn't know her, they have no medical records on her, but there is a concern that she may be suffering from dementia. She was non-communicative with the ER staff. They couldn't really determine what was wrong with her. They got her hydrated and stabilized, but then she just disappeared. We are afraid she may be out there someplace in need of help, and we wonder if there is any chance that she has been in contact with you, or come back to this place that was once her home."

Ben's thoughts went to the woman he had seen in the woods while out looking for Bigfoot with Bob Peters. "I only had one experience with her, and that was over at Mountain Properties Realty when we agreed to buy the house."

Tyndall frowned, as if he hadn't heard correctly. "Where did you say?"

"Mountain Properties Realty," said Ben.

Officer Tyndall glanced over at his partner, Officer Yates, to get his reaction, and all he got was a head-shake. "Is that office open again?" Tyndall asked Ben, though it was more of a rhetorical question as Ben had no knowledge of the history of the place.

Ben recalled that day he met Mrs. Breedlove at the realtor's office. "The place didn't look very open," he said. "I met with the property owner and the realtor there and the place was dark and dusty. It didn't look like a functioning business."

"I'd be surprised if it is," said Officer Tyndall. "That company was shut down years ago over some sort of a property scandal. I was just a kid around here at the time, and don't know much about it, but I recall that it was big news locally. The guy who ran the place was apparently involved in some sort of title fraud, or was in cahoots with a crooked title company, or something like that."

"That sounds right," said Officer Yates. "I remember something about that. My mom used to work at that dry cleaners right next door to that realty office, so I would be around there sometimes as a kid, and I remember getting into that building after the realty was shut down. I shouldn't be saying that, probably, because we weren't supposed to be in there, but I recall that the place was not doing business, it was closed and dark. That was twenty years ago."

The two officers talked with Ben for a time, and he assured them that his only contact with Mrs. Breedlove was that one day at the realtor's office. A purchasing package had been put together, which Ben and Joanna had signed and delivered back to Mountain Properties Realty, and that had been it. There was no mortgage, so nobody held a title, though Ben and Joanna had paid title insurance. That title search and the rest of it had all been closed and the deed was in the hands of Ben and Joanna, which they figured meant that the farm was theirs, end of story.

"I don't know that this is anything," said Ben, "but I was out walking in the forest a couple days ago and I believe I saw an old woman there. I thought it might have been Mrs. Breedlove, though I have only seen her the one time so wasn't sure."

"You saw a woman in the woods?" ask Officer Tyndall. "When and where was this?"

"Just the day before yesterday in the woods, right here behind our property," said Ben. "We tried to catch up with her…"

"Who's we?" asked Tyndall.

"The newspaper guy, Bob Peters was with me," said Ben. "He saw her, too."

"What was he doing back there?" asked the officer.

"We were looking for Bigfoot tracks," said Ben, a comment that inspired the two cops to glance at each other. Ben noticed and could only imagine what the glance must mean. "I had reported seeing these tracks, so the newspaper guy came out to have a look."

"What did you show him?" asked Officer Tyndall.

"I took some photographs that were useless, so I took him back into the woods to try to find these tracks, and we couldn't find anything," said Ben.

"But you saw Mrs. Breedlove?" asked Tyndall.

"I saw an old woman who might have been Mrs. Breedlove," said Ben.

"But you didn't report this?" asked the officer.

"I didn't think to report it," said Ben. "I wasn't aware that she was missing. We did try to catch up with her to ask if she needed help, but we never found her."

Tyndall looked at his fellow officer. "We better get a search party out into those woods," he said, and the officer then walked off the porch and back toward their patrol car, saying something into a radio mic as he walked. Ben couldn't hear what he was saying.

Officer Tyndall took Ben's cell phone number and asked that he contact him should he have any further contact with Mrs. Breedlove. The officers left to arrange a search group that scoured the woods the rest of the day without success. If that was Mrs. Breedlove who Ben and Bob Peters had seen in the woods, she didn't seem to be there now, at least not that the police could find.

That night, however, Ben got a call from Officer Tyndall. "I thought you might be interested to know that I did a little further checking on Mountain Properties Realty," the officer told Ben. "That company is not licensed to sell real estate, so I don't know what that means about the legitimacy of your property purchase. You might want to consult an attorney. And here is the other part that is really interesting. The scandal that got that realtor tossed out of the industry all had to do with your property – yours and the one just up the road from you. Those properties were both the subject of real estate shenanigans and that is why that road out to your house is private. The city never approved an extension of the maintained roadway system out to your place because it was apparently never considered a legal property."

Ben hung up from the call stunned.

He looked at Joanna, who was watching him and sensing that something was wrong. "That was the police officer who was here earlier. He has been looking into the history of the property transactions involving this place, and he isn't sure it was ever Mrs. Breedlove's to sell."

"What?" said Joanna in disbelief. "I knew I should have managed that whole thing! So, what does this mean?"

"I don't know," said Ben, shaking his head. "I have no idea."

*

That night, neither Ben nor Joanna could sleep. They stayed up as late as they could, talking about what they had learned that day and considering what could conceivably come of it and what they should do. After finally feeling settled in their new home, they were suddenly thrown right back into a feeling of limbo, as if everything they felt they had gained could suddenly be taken from them.

It hit Joanna hard. In the short time that they had been on the Goat Farm, she had completely immersed herself in the place. She had come to feel every inch of it in her soul, even her loins. It was spiritually hers – Ben's and hers – whatever legal obstacles may arise. Maybe there would be none, that was all she could hope. But whatever, she was here and this is where she was staying.

Ben was less certain because he always expected the worst, which wasn't without strategy. He had this way of looking at life that suggested that every upturn and downturn was a revelation, and it was always his idea to ride those revelations and turn them into stories. Ben expected weirdness, even wished for it, and if the next weird thing to happen was that they would lose the Goat Farm over a real estate snafu, that would make quite a piece!

*

This evening it was Ben who finally drifted to sleep first, leaving Joanna to sit up alone, staring out into the night.

The moon wasn't full, but the night was cloudless and bright. Joanna sat downstairs until after midnight, thinking, reading a little, and smoking. She then went about the task of turning off lights downstairs, preparing to join Ben in bed to try to get some rest for the night. But as she switched off the last downstairs light she noticed something reflecting brightly in the yard, an ethereal form in the moonlight.

It was an old woman, dressed in white, and she was standing on the redwood deck overlooking the lagoon. She had long white hair, falling past her shoulders on down her back, and she seemed to glow in the light, like a luminous, ethereal being.

Joanna stepped out onto the front porch, watching the form by the lagoon, who seemed oblivious to her presence. Stepping off the porch, Joanna quietly moved up the little trail that led to the deck, careful with each step not to alarm whoever or whatever was there.

Joanna's pulse was racing, her heart pounding as she climbed up onto the deck and moved slowly around to the woman's left side, watching her closely, careful and dead quiet.

The woman was ancient, with pale skin deeply lined with crevices and wrinkles. Her long, thin nose hooked dramatically, as if pulled by gravity over centuries, until finally it aimed down, toward the underworld.

"Mrs. Breedlove?" Joanna whispered. "Are you Mrs. Breedlove?" she asked gently.

The old woman was wearing a hospital gown, open in the back, exposing her buttocks and thighs, papered with skin so thin that it appeared like crepe, blue in the light of the moon.

"I've been out to the meadow," said the old woman, speaking as if in a trance. "The stones don't glow for me anymore. Nobody comes. I thought if I came back…"

Her thoughts trailed as she stared down into the waters of the lagoon.

"They took him," she said, "those evil, awful girls. Dragged him down, took him under. They let him serve his purpose and then they took him down where they go - the goblins."

Joanna looked at her, not knowing quite what to do.

"Mrs. Breedlove, come inside and let me get you under a blanket or into some clothes," said Joanna, speaking cautiously, almost whispering. "You must be cold".

She looked at Mrs. Breedlove's bare feet and wondered at how she had gotten out to the Goat Farm, so far from town, and from the hospital.

"You don't know at first," said Mrs. Breedlove, her eyes fixed on the lagoon. "The flute, playing in my mind, even now. And the sex. I didn't know, until it was too late. They'll take your husband and they'll take you. You'll know by the goats, goats everywhere, poor little dears. They need tending but they go bad."

And with that, Mrs. Breedlove walked right off the deck, landing in the lagoon with a splash, and she disappeared under the water.

"Mrs. Breedlove!" yelled Joanna, rushing to the side of the lagoon, peering into the waters. "Mrs. Breedlove!" she cried, but the old woman was gone, gone below.

CHAPTER 34

Joanna rushed back to the house and called for emergency services. It took nearly twenty minutes for police, ambulance, and a fire truck to show up.

Joanna reported what had happened: that a lady she believed to be Lita Breedlove had showed up on the Goat Farm, uttered some cryptic remarks about her dead husband, and then disappeared into the waters of the lagoon.

Police and fire fighters searched the waters and the island at its center for more than an hour before finding nothing and giving up.

An officer took a detailed report from Joanna, but around 2 a.m. the entire contingent left uncertain that anything had actually happened at the Goat Farm.

"That lady is a pothead, I could smell it on her clothes," one officer reported to another, and that became a part of the report. They could find nothing to show that the missing Mrs. Breedlove was ever at the Goat Farm that night. There was no evidence of any kind. How this woman, whose exact age was also a mystery, but who was at least in her eighties, had traveled on foot, wearing only a hospital gown, from downtown Grass Valley out to this remote location was impossible to imagine.

"So, what do we do with this?" asked one officer to another. "How do we classify our report?"

"I'm not sure, X-File maybe," said his commanding officer.

"Until Mrs. Breedlove's body shows up somewhere, we have to assume she is still just missing and needs to be found. The case remains open. As for what we say about the potheads at the Goat Farm, I'm not even sure it matters. Write up what the wife said and file it. I don't see that we have anything else we can do. Keep it in mind as a strange aspect of the Breedlove story."

CHAPTER 35

"So tell me about your novel," said Joanna.

"I'm not sure I want to talk about it yet," said Ben.

"Tell me about *The Whore of Baphomet*," said Joanna.

"Why don't you tell me about The Whore of Baphomet," said Ben, motioning toward her crafts project. "You seem to have had the intuitive inspiration to call up such a reference. Where did that come from?"

"I don't know," said Joanna. After pausing for a long moment, she asked – "Did you ever wish that we had children, like normal people?"

Ben looked at her, flummoxed. "Where the hell did that come from? You know I don't like kids."

"You are on a goat farm," said Joanna.

It took Ben a second. "Right, I see what you did there. Kids, baby goats, I get it. But why are we talking about this?"

"I don't know," said Joanna. "Maybe it's this place. The whole fucking thing…"

"I wish you wouldn't talk that way," said Ben, "you know it bothers me."

"Sorry, sorry, it's just that the whole fucking place somehow screams sex to me," said Joanna.

"Oh, well, in that context, I guess all the vulgar language is called for," said Ben, shaking his head in false resignation, then – "I saw two people fucking in the woods yesterday."

"What?"

"When I was out wandering around with Peters," said Ben. "We came over a hill and there they were, flagrante delicto in the sex hole, right there in the woods."

"On our property?"

"Yeah, I think so," said Ben. "I'm unclear about the property lines. Peters said we have to watch out for pot growers back there."

"That's what we should do," said Joanna.

"What, grow pot?"

"Have sex in the woods," said Joanna.

"Yeah, right – I think those days are behind us," said Ben.

"Yeah, well, speak for yourself, fuck-head," said Joanna, grinning mischievously.

That should piss him off.

CHAPTER 36

"Show me where you saw Bigfoot," said Joanna.

Ben grimaced. "I'm no longer sure I saw anything," he said. "I thought I did, there were tracks, but without proof…"

"Well, then, show me where you saw those people having sex."

"Why, for God's sake?" asked Ben.

Joanna shrugged. "I'm just curious."

"It was in the woods, in a ravine, sort of tucked away," said Ben. "I doubt I can even find it again."

"Show me," said Joanna.

*

Ben and Joanna walked for thirty minutes or so back into the forest, Ben looking anxiously around the entire way, falling repeatedly, trying to find something that looked familiar, or some marker in the woods that he might find again on their way back. It was a faint hope. Everything walking one direction looked different than it did walking in the opposite direction, so experience with the path – not that there was one – was a poor teacher. Aboriginal people, native to the area, had developed an innate sense of direction and didn't have to rely on visual markers alone. Ben had no pathfinder skills. Far from being a Natty Bumpo, he could hardly make it safely to the bathroom at night.

Joanna didn't seem to care that she wasn't with an Eagle Scout.

She followed along behind Ben, taking in the fragrance of the forest, rich with deep aromatic smells accented by minty flavors and jasmine. She strode confidently along over difficult terrain, as if born to the tall redwoods, the pine, and the spruce. The theater she walked through was a cathedral of ornate and mysterious emerald beauty, with powerful vines hanging from branches, wrapping around trunks and limbs, hugging them as opportunistic invaders, the Ent all around subjugated by these snake gods, captive to their strangulating grips.

By some miracle, they eventually came to a spot that Ben declared to be their destination. He was not one-hundred percent sure that he was at the right place, but he began to doubt that he could ever be that sure about anything in these woods, so he declared this the place. "This is where I was standing when I saw what I believe to be a Sasquatch, and right over here there were prints that I took photographs of."

"Yeah, I don't care about any of that," said Joanna. "Where were the people fucking?"

"What is with you and this fucking thing?" said Ben. "And I wish you would stop talking that way. It's not attractive."

"Maybe not to you," said Joanna. "Some people like a girl with a potty mouth. I could show you."

"What is wrong with you!" said Ben. "Come on, I'll show you the fucking ravine."

Over the next ten minutes they trekked the path that Peters and Ben had taken back from their Bigfoot non-sighting, to the spot where they had encountered the amorous couple.

"I suppose you are hoping they will still be there," said Ben, peaking over the top of the hill into the ravine, just in case.

Joanna walked over the top of the hill, grabbed Ben's hand, and pulled him along with her as she slid down into the deep ravine, where there flowed a small seasonal stream and trees had fallen across the divide. At the bottom she began removing her clothes.

"Is this the place?"

"What are you doing?" asked Ben, alarmed.

"I feel like a wood nymph," said Joanna, removing her jeans, revealing her nakedness.

"A nymph of some kind!" said Ben, alarmed. "What is wrong with you?"

"What is wrong with you?" asked Joanna, pulling her sweater over her head, becoming totally nude.

"You remember we are here because I saw two people fucking?" asked Ben. "People can see you fucking here!"

"So what?" asked Joanna. "Take off your clothes. Let's get in the water."

"Are you out of your mind?" asked Ben.

Joanna started rubbing the crotch of his jeans and undulating against him, unbuckling his pants, then pulling off his shirt, and undressing him almost before he realized what she was doing. She dropped to her knees before him and took his cock into her mouth, where it began to swell before Ben suddenly pulled away.

"I am not at all comfortable with this," he said, looking at his wife of thirty-three years as if she was someone he had never met before. "Get up, you're going to get ticks on your privates."

Joanna, still kneeling before him, massaging his cock, noticed his legs, white as a deep ocean fish. "You've lost all the hair on your legs," she said.

And as she said that, she thought she heard the sound of laughter from the ridges around them.

"And my chest, too. Did you hear something?" asked Ben, looking around.

"Did you have hair on your chest?" asked Joanna, still kneading his cock, growing flatulent and useless.

Again, the sound of laughter from the woods.

"It won't get hard, will it?" said Joanna.

"Well, not if you are going to comment about my diminishing, lifeless form," said Ben, speaking matter-of-factly while looking nervously around. "It's a prostate condition. It'll probably be the thing that kills me."

And, again, there was laughter.

"Are you not hearing that?" asked Ben.

"Hearing what?" asked Joanna, slowly standing and undulating against him like a snake.

Ben moved away from her and started tugging his clothing back on. "I think we should get out of here," he said.

"Wait, I just have to do this," said Joanna, taking the opportunity of her nudity to lie in the cold mountain stream, letting the water ripple across her body in sensuous patterns.

The current of the waters poured over her, splitting into v-shapes as they touched her erect nipples, standing up out of the clear waters like monuments created in perfect alignment with nature.

CHAPTER 37

Joanna had lost her urge for nicotine.

It hit her little-by-little that she was not getting the benefit from lighting up her Kools the way she always had, sucking in their mint flavor and feeling the deadening that followed, the numbness. That familiar comfort had been hers dating back to when she was a young girl. Somehow her pack-a-day habit hadn't killed her, as it had others in her family. The only downside she had ever experienced was that she couldn't breathe, and she smelled like an ashtray, but weighing the calming of her nerves against those inconveniences had been a no-brainer choice for her until lately.

Lately she found herself reaching for her Kools and lighter out of habit, rather than desire, until it began to feel like a chore, like smoking was something she had been wired to do but that finally held no appeal for her.

Replacing her desire for nicotine was a new obsession with the taste of honey.

One day, in the midst of this realization that smoking wasn't doing for her what it once did – smoking cigarettes, not marijuana, which was still working just fine – Joanna noticed a jar of honey in a kitchen cupboard.

This jar of honey had migrated with them from the Bay Area, and had been opened once long ago and never opened again, and now there was a crystalline build-up around the rim of the jar. It flaked away and fell on the counter as she opened it and peered inside at its golden goodness.

Something about looking into that rich, golden substance made her want to stick a finger deep into it and extract a thick glob of its sugary stickiness.

She stuck her honey-laden finger into her mouth and sucked the nectar clean, and then she stuck two fingers into the jar, and eagerly consumed what she could extract. And she repeated that pattern with a growing, manic relish until finally the level of the supply had fallen so far that she resorted to tipping the jar up and emptying its remaining contents directly into her throat.

This bizarre incident set off an obsession with honey, which became an important item on she and Ben's shopping list. Ben had braced himself for a grocery trip to Grass Valley every ten days or so, which always featured some kind of an incident with Riley Cooter's vicious dogs.

The trips were so painful, that Ben doubled orders of heavily consumed food stuffs, which came to include honey. Joanna would ask him to get four jars of honey, and he would get eight.

"What are you doing with all this honey?" Ben asked, bewildered by the growing need for re-supply.

Joanna didn't bake or use it in cooking. She used it on English Muffins, but it was a mystery to Ben, who never used the stuff, where all this honey could possibly be going.

"Are you drinking this shit?" he asked.

Joanna looked sheepish. "Maybe."

"I don't know what has gotten into you," said Ben, revealing his absolute truth.

Joanna didn't know either. She actually wondered if she wasn't experiencing some sort of a sugar shock, a honey-induced state if euphoria, like a vampire having come into a fresh blood supply. She was feeling a vitality like she had never felt before. Her skin glowed, her muscles toned, and areas that may once have sagged now pulled taut, as if toned for battle. Her hair shone with a luster a seal might envy, and she smelled like a butterfly garden.

Surely a part of it was the goat milk, which was another item that had been added to the regular shopping list. Joanna had forsaken cow's milk for the milk of goats, which she consumed voraciously.

Another thing changed, as well.

"Are you not smoking?" asked Ben. It was obvious to him that she had simply stopped, but her habit had been so cemented into her character that he could hardly believe this new experience. He found that his allergies, which were always inflamed, became less bothersome. Their whole house smelled better, as if recovering from a period of plague. Now the worse that could be said about it was that it smelled a little too sweet. There was all this honey everywhere, but there was also the smell of flowering plants that seemed to grow more profound around the Goat Farm every day. Ben wondered if it didn't seem so noticeable because the nicotine obstruction of his senses was gone, so now he could pick up on aromas previously lost to his battered olfactories.

"I have stopped smoking," confirmed Joanna.

"And you are okay with it?" asked Ben. "You were smoking in the womb, weren't you?"

"Yes, if by womb you mean high school," said Joanna.

"Wow, think how long ago that was!" enthused Ben.

Joanna winced at his insensitivity. "Yeah, well, fuck you," said Joanna. "You're older than I am."

"But I never smoked, see!" said Ben. "That's why I am such a wonder to behold today."

His crestfallen irony was apparent. He looked like a misshapen foot and she looked like Helen of Troy. What the fuck is going on here? Ben didn't say that aloud, but that's what he was thinking.

That's what Joanna was wondering, too.

*

There were beehives on the state park property bordering the north side of the Goat Farm.

Joanna discovered them one day, drawn to them as if summoned by some invisible force; locked in a trance by an aroma that infiltrated her nostrils and grabbed hold of her senses, setting her on a journey.

She could hear the sounds of bees as if she were in the midst of a nest. She closed her eyes and she could see them, all around her, working away at the surrounding cells, sealed tight with pure honey.

Joanna had begun to drool.

She had been standing in the kitchen when the scent hit her, and her mouth immediately filled with drool and before she realized what was happening a flood of it ran down her chin and plopped upon the floor.

It was honey. She could taste the honey.

Ben was in the next room, in his ridiculous little cubby, lost in his ridiculous little thoughts, unaware that his wife, who seemed to be growing more lubricious daily, was salivating like a heated whore.

Joanna walked out the front door of the house, crossed the porch and walked on out into the yard, and she kept going.

Neither she nor Ben had ever explored the property on the north side of the gated entry to the Goat Farm. The road ended at their property, and there was a tall row of shrubberies and trees that walled off Sherwood Forest from their farm. It was a daunting barrier that a person would need a powerful reason to attempt to cross, but Joanna seemed so empowered.

She pushed her way through the bushes and waded through blackberry vines that cut her arms and legs as she went.

Joanna had taken to wearing dresses. This was another of the changes that had come over her, because she had never felt comfortable in a dress. She hated the objectification of women. Her idol was the rock warrior Chrissie Hynde, and her typical attire was more sweatshirt and jeans than feminizations of any kind. Of late, sartorial change had washed over her like unpasteurized honey. She took to wearing dresses that to Ben seemed to materialize from thin air. He had never seen most of these things before. They were vintage dresses Joanna had acquired in her youth, when she had worked for a time at a modeling agency and was encouraged to dress less like a man.

Joanna favored loose dresses, that buttoned down the front with a plunging neckline, and that were cut at knee length, revealing her sturdy legs. She was not tall and until recently had always hated what she referred to as her "peasant legs", which like the rest of her had shaped in admirable ways since she had come to the Goat Farm, and particularly since she'd gone on her strange honey diet.

She had pushed her way through the bushes, trees, and brambles, not sure of what was drawing her through this gauntlet but never thinking of stopping. There was something out there ahead that she had to get to.

It came clear as she suddenly thrashed her way into a clearing, where she saw two long rows of little white structures. Somebody was keeping bees back there in Sherwood Forest, probably illegally.

Joanna had entered the clearing and begun walking from one bee enclosure to the next, unmindful of the honeybees that swarmed all around her, checking her closely but not landing on her, not stinging.

She could smell the rich honey and the drool kept coming, causing her to wipe at the corners of her mouth constantly as she moved among the little forest of bee huts.

In the middle of the colony she came upon a house that had been laid open, possibly by a bear?

Joanna peered inside and she could see the honeycomb formations that had been built in perfect hexagonal cells so that each rack within the enclosure looked like a bee apartment building.

She reached in to touch one of the honeycombs, curious as to what it must feel like, and when she did she accidentally pierced the propolis shell covering one honey-filled cell and she watched as the pure stuff dripped down the wall of cells. She used her finger to capture some of the honey and she tasted it.

It was warm and sweet. She punctured another cell and got another finger full of the pure stuff. Phytonutrients coursed through her veins, flooding her with bacterial-viral-and-fungus fighting enzymes. It flushed any cancer that Joanna may have had developing within her system. A tumor on her back, that she had always thought of as a barely noticeable fat deposit, disappeared in the following weeks, and she developed such strength as she had never had before.

As Joanna poked through another propolis cover, the rack of honeycomb fell from the corrupted hive house and landed on the ground at her feet. Bees went crazy, swarming around her in a buzzing cloud, but Joanna didn't notice. She knelt and picked up the rack of honeycomb.

There were dead bees in some of the cells, and live bees crawled over the honeycomb and walked up her arm as she held the rack.

Joanna poked more holes in the propolis covers and consumed the pure honey contained within those cells, and then she turned and sat on the ground, leaning against the broken hive house.

Honey dripped from the rack. She held it above her head, positioning herself beneath the ribbons of gold that dripped from the combs, some going into her mouth, but more landing on her face, neck, and shoulders.

The sticky glue ran into her hair and her dress, weighting the thin fabric until it sagged heavy with sweetness, opening the front and revealing a nipple. The honey ran down Joanna's chin and onto her chest and on down her stomach, warm and sticky, searching her crevices.

Dead bees came with the rain of gold, and they stuck to her skin, crawling down her in a slow motion death parade as the honey flowed down her body.

It was in her crotch, on her thighs – everywhere. She reached down and swept a handful from her groin and wiped it across her face, continuing to pour honey from the comb that she held above her head.

No bees stung her.

They circled her, landing on her occasionally as if to sense her more deeply, to check her out, but they seemed to accept her.

She was a sticky queen, or a sticky goddess, or a sticky whore.

She was sticky, that's all that was apparent. And she was in an ecstatic state, and she remained that way for some time, taking in the nectar from this strange wooded source, and from these obliging bees.

When she had finally had enough, they followed her out of the clearing, seeing her through the blackberries, the bushes and the vines, until finally she was back to her house.

There they left her on the porch, as she stepped inside.

Ben walked out of his writing room about the time that Joanna came into the living room.

"What in the hell happened to you?" he asked, staring at her in worried amazement.

She looked, to his mind, like that girl Carrie in that creepy movie where they dumped pig blood on her, except that Joanna just looked otherworldly, not a victim of horror, but possibly one of some horrible House of Pancakes accident.

Her hair was matted, her skin glowed with a rich dew, and her dress clung tight to her body, accentuating a renewed form that of late had taken on noticeably dangerous curves.

"I found a beehive colony," said Joanna.

"Oh," said Ben, a little afraid of what that might mean. "Did you do something to it?"

"What?" asked Joanna, not understanding.

"You have bees stuck to you," said Ben. "I hope those things aren't alive." No sooner had he said that than he considered the uncomfortable alternative.

Joanna looked down at one of the bees stuck to her partially exposed breast. She pulled it from her skin and examined it, lifeless between her thumb and index finger.

"They're dead," she confirmed to Ben, who stood looking at his wife, utterly at a loss to comprehend her condition.

She was in a state of some kind. He couldn't tell if it was bliss or trauma.

She was sticky, dirty, and unbelievably beautiful, like a sexed starlet having just come from a casting call on the Honey King's couch.

CHAPTER 38

Joanna rode her forest stranger hard over the next weeks.

She would slip out to the meadow while Ben was lost in his weird writer dreams, pounding away at the keys of his machine unaware that Joanna was out pounding nature. She would go to the meadow and give herself to the rude aggressions of the forest stranger, and be roughed by him, and enjoy passions free of physical harm, beyond the overwhelming strength of her own orgasms.

Every time felt like a surrender to an irresistible force, a thing she allowed to happen with knowledge of her own culpability for what felt a lot like rape, and which immunized her from shame or guilt. She couldn't seem to help that she was being used like a whore – like the Whore of Baphomet – by some subhuman creature from the woods. And she found freedom in the way her thoughts would leave her, when the breeze moved a certain way, and that jasmine smell would be all around. And in the way the sun felt on her naked skin, and the way those granite stones enveloped her whole body with a soothing warmth.

She would lose herself in his physical form, her mind and will disconnecting from her own corporeal self in a way that let her feel free to take him all in – his taste, power, and smell.

CHAPTER 39

The women who had been drawn to the Goat Farm had all been women who had never given birth to children.

Having children creates particular sensitivities within a woman. Mothers tune into frequencies and messages otherwise hidden to women who have never gone through their same portal, which entered them into another reality, different from that of their native state.

Women who have not brought life into this world have a frequency of their own, and it is strong. Where the mother's energies increase with the size of their fold, it is an energy that is dissipated, distributed in her world in amounts that she carefully measures and monitors. It is part of how she communicates fairness and a sense of right and wrong to her young.

She who has not given to the world in that way exists as a battery, her bottled energies creating a special frequencty of their own, with receptors that capture another unique set of signals from the universe. Those who care for children in the real world are fairly grounded in Gaia. Those who do not may feel the influences of other realms.

Joanna was one of those. The Goat Farm opened her up in ways that unleashed her energies, and in that release she saw the beings of her elemental world - the creatures from her imagination that she made real, that explained her way of feeling about things, and about the choices she made. They came to her in forms that satisfied those parts of her child's mind that she still remembered with delight. The faeries and elves. They came to her when she was lost in the stone meadow, liberating them with those bottled up energies that she released from within herself. They were beautiful and kind, seemingly almost worshipful of her. And then there had been the other.

Indeed, there was something special about Joanna, beyond her lack of experience with childbirth. After all, Guita was childless and had come to the meadow, and her experience had been totally different.

Where must her energies be going?

CHAPTER 40

Joanna had come to the stone meadow, which had its usual effect. Her mind and her body relaxed, and she grew sleepy. As she lingered there, waiting for whatever would happen next, she fell asleep on one of the altar stones.

She hadn't been asleep long when she felt a presence, and she opened her eyes to see a young boy sitting cross-legged across the stone from her, grinning at her.

Joanna sat up, alarmed, and said – "Who are you?"

The kid, who looked to be about twelve or thirteen, had a babyish face framed by curly hair that grew artfully around his ears and the back side of his head. It created a halo effect, as least as Joanna saw it. It was late afternoon and he was backlit by the sun. He was handsome, with striking eyes, almost golden. His ears protruded and folded in a way that lent an elfin quality to his look.

"Willie," he answered.

Joanna pushed herself off the stone and stood up, facing him. "Are you aware that you are on my property?" she asked, not in an accusatory way, but more like she was being careful with a young person.

The kid grinned – "You weren't born here. I was."

"You were born here?" she asked. The thought flashed in her mind that this is also what her forest stranger had claimed. "Do you live nearby? Who are your parents?"

"I live around," and he nodded back toward the forest.

"With your parents?" asked Joanna. "Those are also my woods."

The kid chuckled. "I've seen you having sex with Veebo."

Joanna looked shocked. She felt her defenses rise and she stepped back a bit. "I don't know what you are talking about," said Joanna.

"He used to have sex with the old woman who lived here," said the kid. "Veebo will fuck anything," he said in wonder, shaking his head. Then he immediately thought about what that implied. "I didn't mean that you are just anything," he said. "You aren't like the old lady, you're special, I can see that."

Joanna was beginning to feel uncomfortable in ways she had never felt in the stone meadow before. "Look, kid, I don't know who you are, but I think you should go on home."

"I told you, my name is Willie," he said. "And I am home. It's more my home than yours. You've only been here a few weeks."

"I bought the fucking place," said Joanna.

Willie made a face. "I'm just a kid, but I don't think it works that way."

Joanna was losing patience. "It works that way, it's called a real estate transaction, now you really need to go home."

Willie looked hurt, but undaunted. "You don't have to be mean, I'm not really doing anything to you, just talking."

"Yeah, well I don't like the things you are saying," said Joanna, "and I really want to be left here alone."

"Waiting for Veebo?" asked Willie, grinning.

Joanna winced. "Is that his name?"

"Yep, Veebo, that's his name," said Willie. "He's my brother, one of them."

There was a moment of considered silence. "Are we talking

about the same guy?" asked Joanna.

"How many people have been having sex with you here in the meadow?" asked Willie.

A look of horror came over Joanna's face. "Who the hell are you? You've been watching me, like a little fucking pervert?"

That seemed to confuse Willie. "No, I'm just watching."

Joanna raged – "Get the fuck out of here!"

Just as she did, her forest stranger rushed at her unseen, hitting into her like she was a tackling dummy and rolling her across the grass.

He was stark naked, with an erection the size of a prize carrot, and without hesitation Joanna got up and punched him in his grapefruit nuts and then grabbed onto them like she was crushing croutons.

"What the fuck is wrong with you!" she snarled up at him.

Veebo's eyes shot open wide and he let out such a scream that Ben heard it at his writing desk and rushed to the front porch. "Joanna!" he yelled into the farmyard. "Are you okay?"

Joanna had a hold of Veebo's nuts with a strength beyond any she had ever summoned before, and the big man paled, and shriveled, too. His arrested penis melted into its wooly pouch as its owner whimpered like a dog bitten by a merciless bitch. "Don't you ever fucking touch me again, you understand!" she said, gnashing her teeth as she issued a threat. "I will fucking tear your nuts off and stick them down your throat!"

With that she let go and Veebo made a hasty retreat to the woods, dragging one leg as if Joanna's perfectly calibrated attack had paralyzed a part of him.

Willie started laughing his head off, falling over backwards on the stone, rolling around and holding his stomach, his abs in pain with the violence of his amusement.

"That's your brother?" asked Joanna.

"Yeah, he's an idiot," Willie said through his laughter.

"What kind of a family do you come from?" asked Joanna, not really wanting to know.

"Yours, now," said Willie.

Joanna looked at him, agitated. "What do you mean by that?"

"You'll see," said Willie, laughing. "You'll see!"

Joanna had heard enough. "Get off my property, Willie!" And then she turned and stomped away, leaving the stone meadow and heading back to the house. There she found Ben, calling her name, but not coming off the porch.

"Are you okay?" he asked. "Where did you go?"

"I'm fine," said Joanna, still agitated.

He thought to ask what she was upset about, but inside, on his laptop, was a section of his book that was going so well that he didn't want to stop to listen to what he suspected was some passing pique. She got that way, getting an attitude over something that bothered her for reasons she wouldn't share, and then it would pass. Ben had learned not to react, even knowing that Joanna often took that as him just not caring about her.

The rest of that afternoon she spent on the deck overlooking the lagoon, thinking about what Willie had said; thinking about everything that had happened since she first walked into the meadow.

CHAPTER 41

One of the first places that Joanna had noticed when she and Ben moved into the area were all the signs advertising psychic and Tarot Card readings. It seemed like Nevada County was full of these people and many of them had wonderfully creative signs advertising their services.

Joanna was particularly taken by a sign she saw hanging from the front porch of one of Nevada City's classic Victorians. Around since California's Gold Rush era, they populate the villages along the Gold Country foothills like ornate gravestones commemorating that earlier time.

There was a psychic living in Nevada City in a beautiful old Victorian, gray-brown with off-white trim, and doors and shutters painted deep green, so the whole thing blended seamlessly into its leafy environs.

Her name was Beverly Bolin, though her signage read "Readings by Madame B" and it featured the image of a friendly cartoon goat. There were two hands cupped around what appeared to be a scrying ball, and behind that was this goat looking on in a comically interested way, and he had the eye of Horus. This was all done on a dark blue background, the color of psychic sensitivity. The cupped hands and scrying ball appeared to be professionally silk-screened while the goat appeared to have been painted by an untalented five-year old.

Joanna found the overall effect to be oddly welcoming – exactly the right blend of hoodoo and humorous perspective. She wasn't sure how the goat fit in, but judging from the sign, she felt that she could take Madame B seriously, not only as a psychic, but possibly also as comic entertainment. At least that's what she told herself, but in truth she was desperate to know what had come over her that she was having crazy sex with some guy she wasn't even sure wasn't an animal. She would welcome any kind of comic relief that would take the edge off that while probing for good information to explain the unexplainable.

Madame B met her at the door and welcomed her into her finely maintained home, which was a warehouse of museum quality lace. The whole place looked like a demonstration model for a home built in 1849, a display intended to show interested parties what it looked like back when people had class.

Plus, Madame B's 19th Century spiritualism benefited greatly from staging within a home of that period. The whole scene looked and smelled like Madame Blavatsky's parlor.

Madame B escorted Joanna back to a drawing room off the main living room – all the furnishings in the place were period correct, sized to the dimensions of the multi-roomed design that left little in the way of open wall space.

They tucked themselves around a small circular table, and when both were comfortable Madame B lowered the lights in the room and removed a black scarf, revealing the scrying ball advertised on her ridiculous sign.

It was a good ball, top quality, apparently shaped from quartz crystal, but it was a pretty blue. There appeared to be clouds within it, which Joanna thought she saw move, noting to herself that this was a pretty good trick. If you were going to claim to have psychic insight into people's personal lives it is certainly helpful to have a good scrying ball. A cheap scrying ball would be a dead giveaway, or so Joanna reasoned, though she had never had previous personal experience with the subject. She felt confident that Madame B had.

"Okay, let us start by learning a little bit about you," said Madame B in a comforting voice.

She looked a little like a gypsy. She was probably fifty years old and she had dark wavy hair that fell past her shoulders. She wore a headband with a moon and star pattern, which Joanna felt was a nice touch, and she had on a lot of eye makeup, so she was a little spooky to look at.

"What I would like for you to do is just relax yourself, rest your elbows on the table, and without touching the scrying ball I would like for you to position your hands to either side," instructed Madame B. "In a comfortable position, I just want you to position your hands so that your palms are facing the ball. And I want you to close your eyes, and…"

Madame B gasped. "Holy shit! You bought the Goat Farm!"

Shocked, Joanna quickly pulled her hands away from the ball and pushed herself back from the table.

"Oh my god," said Madame B, flustered and embarrassed. "Sorry, sorry, that was totally unprofessional of me. I so apologize. My license should be revoked! The curse of the pharaohs should be placed upon me!"

"How did you know that?" said Joanna, alarmed. "How did you know that about the Goat Farm?"

Madame B's eyes darted around like her brain was on overload. "Well, you placed your hands around the crystal and I just immediately saw you on the Goat Farm, and you were doing," she struggled, lost for words before finally coming up with "things".

Joanna's mouth dropped open. "That's horrible!" she shrieked. "What are you doing looking into my private life like that?"

Madame B struck a comical thinking pose, as if the question was too much for her little brain. "Geez, I don't know, maybe because I'm a psychic and you came for a psychic reading?"

The two stopped and stared at each other for a moment, unsure what to do next, then Madame B broke the freeze.

"Okay, we got off on the wrong foot," she said, stepping over to the doorway and flipping the light switch, re-illuminating the room. She tossed the black cover over the scrying ball, saying "I think we've had enough of that. Let's start over and I'll see if I can save this session."

"What do you know about the Goat Farm?" asked Joanna, settling herself back down.

"I know the lady who I thought still owned the place," said Madame B.

"Lita Breedlove?" asked Joanna.

"Lita Breedlove," confirmed Madame B.

"She's dead," said Joanna, matter-of-factly.

Madame B looked at her with surprise, and she immediately ripped the cover back off her scrying ball and stared into it for a moment. She shook her head, then got up and switched off the overhead light once again so she could peer into her device. "Sure as shit," she said, which was intended only for herself but was clearly heard by Joanna. "She's not there anymore, I can see that," said Madame B, brows furrowed, shaking her head.

"She drowned," said Joanna. "She drowned in our lagoon."

Madame B looked up from her scrying and shook her head. "No, she isn't dead, I can see her right here. She's somewhere else, but she's not dead."

"What?" asked Joanna, "Let me see" and she walked around to the side of the table where Madame B had reseated.

Joanna peered into the ball, but she didn't see a thing, beyond that weird gray cloud that seemed to float around inside the orb. "I don't see anything at all," she said, mumbling to herself in her own way, rather like Madame B.

Madame B looked up at her and said - "What, you think anybody can do this? It takes certain sensitivities."

"How do you know Mrs. Breedlove?" asked Joanna.

"She came to me for readings," said Madame B. "That started a long while back, when her husband was still around."

"Still alive, you mean?" asked Joanna.

"Still around," said Madame B. "Wherever Lita's gone to, he's there, too. I don't know where it is, but for better or for worse those two are back together."

*

Lita's marriage to Tom Breedlove hadn't been a storybook romance. Quite the opposite, he had been an abusive husband and for years after they were married, they struggled to survive.

He had been a farm boy from the Stockton area, and she was a local girl who worked the fountain at a local drug store. That's where the two met.

Tom Breedlove was a number of years older than Lita, and when they met, he was working the farmland that his grandfather and father had farmed before him.

It didn't go well. Tom and Lita were married, but the abuses started immediately, growing worse as Tom's fortunes faltered. Lita had stopped working when they were married, but as income from the farm deteriorated to nothing Lita was forced to go back to her old job at the soda fountain.

She had been there by herself one late afternoon, getting ready to clean up the equipment and close for the day, when a strange man came in, sat at the counter, and ordered a Cherry Coke.

"I'm looking for someone," he told her.

"Well, I know pretty much everyone around here," said Lita, "what's this person's name."

"It doesn't matter," said the stranger. "It's not a name I'm looking for, but a person."

"A person?" asked Lita. "What kind of person?"

"A person with a special fire, who wants to bring a special energy," said the man.

"To what?" asked Lita.

"To a property that I have, which I can offer to the right person at a good price," said the man. "It's a straight cash purchase, no contingencies."

"You are a real estate salesman," summed Lita.

"Yes," said the man.

"So, you are just looking for anyone who might have the money and interest in buying a property?" asked Lita.

"And so much more," said the real estate man.

"What do you mean?" asked Lita.

"Security, wellness, a chance to live forever," he said.

"Live forever?" said Lita, smiling, like it was a joke

"A chance to make a real contribution," said the realtor.

Lita frowned, skeptical. "And what kind of money does it take to get this living forever deal, and all this wellness."

"The money is negotiable for the right person," he said.

"And that right person would be?"

"It could be you, Lita," he said, reading her name off the name tag she wore on her waitress uniform.

She shook her head. "No, it couldn't be me," she said, "I don't have any money."

"Like I said," the realtor replied, "it's not just about the money. It is about finding someone right for this property. It is a very special place, beautiful year around. It is bordered by deep, natural forests, and the air is fresh and clear."

"Yeah, well, like I said, I can't afford anything like that," said Lita.

"Well let me ask you a question," said the realtor. "What would you be willing to do to get such a place?"

Lita backed away from him suspiciously. "Okay, you are sounding a little creepy now. What do you mean, what would I be willing to do?"

The realtor narrowed his eyes, considering her potential. "Do you like children, Lita?" he asked.

"Oh no, what are you thinking?" asked Lita. "Are you looking for some kind of a surrogate or something? I'm not interested in being anyone's baby momma. I got a baby at home now, except that he's fifty-six years old and not worth a plug nickel."

"Well, you could save him," said the realtor. "Save him and yourself, set you both up real nice."

Lita shook her head. "Why are you telling me this, what's your angle?"

"I think, from the little time that we have spent here talking, that I have found the person I've come looking for," said the realtor. "Might you be ready to change your life, Lita?"

"Fuck yes!" she said, blurting it out and then looking around the drug store to see if anyone might have snuck in and heard her impropriety. They were alone.

"Then I think I have a deal for you," said the realtor. "There's just one other thing that I have to ask. I have to know that you'll be committed to our arrangement. I've got to know that you can commit to a vision and see it through, because the world needs people like you, Lita. The world needs your energy."

Lita just looked at him, frowning. "Who the fuck are you?" she asked.

"Who are you, Lita?" said the realtor. "That's the real question. And who do you want to be? If you answer that question honestly, and you are interested in the property that I have to offer, then I want you to call me on this number."

The realtor took a business card from his inside coat pocket and placed it on the counter in front of him. "You give this a little thought, Lita. Talk it over with your husband. I sense you two could use a break, and this would be the break of a lifetime."

Lita looked from him to the card. "Okay," she said, "I'll give it some thought."

With that the realtor downed his Cherry Coke and tossed a couple rumpled dollar bills on the counter. He doffed his hat and excused himself, but as he was walking away he stopped and looked back at her.

"One other thing," he said. "How are you with goats?"

CHAPTER 42

Lita Breedlove had picked up that business card and placed the call that had changed her life, just as the realtor had promised.

It was a realty transaction like no other. Lita and her husband put down ten thousand dollars, which they pulled together by selling Tom's ancient farm equipment, and they put Tom's family farm up for sale, selling what was left of what had once been a large spread but that over the years had shrunk in size to just a few acres.

Their move out of the valley and up into the Sierras would be a change of pace, which Lita hoped would calm her husband's raging frustrations, which had turned violent.

Tom was a man-child who became abusive when he drank and over time he drank more and more often. His brutishness was not reserved only for his wife, but rather was a constant feature of his personality and interactions with others. He and Cooter Riley had scrapped almost immediately.

When the Breedloves first moved onto the Goat Farm, Cooter had an old dog that he loved whose name was Rex. Rex was deaf and blind, and Tom Breedlove ran him over with his pickup while he and Lita were moving items to the farm.

Cooter saw the dog get hit. Old Rex often wandered off the farm property to go exploring in the woods on the other side of the road, and he was crossing back over that day that the Breedloves came barreling up the road in their old pickup and hit him.

Tom Breedlove didn't even stop. He felt the bump as the tires of his truck rolled over the old hound, killing him instantly. Cooter had seen the accident and he came running from his house to care for his dog, but there was no life left in him. Rex was dead – as dead as Cooter's late wife – and it crushed his spirit. He jumped in his truck and followed the Breedlove's up the hill to the Goat Farm, and there Cooter and Tom Breedlove had words.

When Cooter returned to his place, he flooded the road in front of his turn-in and then drove a tractor through it. His goal was to create huge ruts that would make impossible, in the future, for any asshole to go barreling up that road. It was a strategy conceived too late to save old Rex, but for damned sure Cooter would own this road in the future.

With their promised new adventure off to a rocky start, Tom began drinking heavily and beating his wife. But then something had happened, something strange in the meadow. A forest stranger appeared and started paying visits to Lita. She would meet him in the meadow and there she would lose herself and forget all about her awful marriage and the brute who held her prisoner in this beautiful setting that had been promised to her as her safe place.

When Tom began abusing their animals a palpable change came over the Goat Farm. There were whispers, undercurrents of strange energies.

Lita could feel the poisoning of the atmosphere, the contamination of the essential purity of their new environment. Then one day Tom waded into the lagoon, convinced that he was hearing strange sounds, seeing strange things, and he wanted to investigate.

Lita had watched him disappear under the water, and watched the bubbles rising from the clear spring as that horrible man went down below, where the goblins go, never to return.

That day marked a major change in the state of affairs at the Goat Farm. Left on her own, Lita threw every ounce of her being into trying to make the farm work, to make it a paying proposition.

She had a herd of goats that was growing in size by the day. As long as she was out in that meadow, being ravaged by the forest stranger, everything seemed to be fine - until it wasn't.

It is a fine line to walk, trying to balance the world on a stone altar. Lita did it for years, a single mother with a huge number of kids.

It took its toll on her. Perhaps, in the end, the realtor had been wrong. Perhaps she hadn't really been the right fit at all.

Lita Breedlove had a fatal flaw: she was human, and she got old, her energies waned until she could no longer be restored.

And one day she went to the meadow and her forest stranger didn't come, and he never came ever again, and with that development things on the Goat Farm began going horribly wrong.

The kids began to come into the world with deformities. They were horrible abominations of what they were meant to be, born into suffering and pain, and Lita sought to relieve their suffering and she began to kill them. She got an axe from the barn and she went from paddock to paddock, separating the well kids from the suffering newborn, which she hacked to death to the horror of their siblings, her well children.

"Lita kills," whispered the wind and then suddenly they were all gone, the healthy as well as the ill-born and the farm was quiet.

She had loved the goats and now they were gone. The silence drove her mad, the emptiness that the space had become, the dark void.

All she had left to recall any of it were the strange drawings that she started finding on her property, collecting in sheaths out in the camping trailer she and Tom had once used for getaways.

It was parked out in the weeds, now. And someone was haunting her with strange images, intricate depictions of goat creatures. They weren't goats and they weren't human, but rather were freakish abominations.

It was a debacle that Lita Breedlove felt responsible for creating. She had failed. With all her heart she had wished to have a wonderful life and be a perfect mother to all her young, but somehow she had failed and she would never understand why.

Some things can't be understood any more than one can understand the nature of cosmic rays beaming onto the altars of our lives from distant heavenly bodies.

CHAPTER 43

1849

"This is it, it's here someplace."

Silenus walked out into the clearing and looked around. "There," he said, pointing toward the edge of the tree line. "And there," he said again, pointing to another spot.

"What are we looking for, Mister Faunus?"

Bert Grimfold was stumped. He had met Silenus Faunus in San Francisco. The older man said he had just arrived from Panama on the new steamer, Hartford, which Allen & Paxson had added to their line to exploit the traffic headed to the gold fields of California. States were organizing expeditions and sending them west, and foreigners were arriving in San Francisco, lured by the promise of riches.

Faunus was a strange character. Tall and thin, he had a sinister look about him. With narrow eyes, upward arching brows, a puckish nose, and pointy ears, he looked rather like an intimidating elf, particularly as his hair grew in ringlets, tight to his head. He always wore a hat, even when he was fucking Bert.

Bert had fallen under Faunus' spell almost immediately upon learning that he was involved in the natural sciences. Bert had a degree in the natural sciences from Bowdin College and he had come west to establish a career as a mining engineer.

In San Francisco, the mining had all been on the part of Mister Faunus, who quickly turned young Bert into his eromenos. When he wasn't boning his new young charge, he was educating him to the nature of a very special mission they were to embark on. They were going to Gold Country.

"There is another one over there," said Silenus, pointing off to the north, "and another over there."

"I don't understand what we are doing," said Bert. "You want to dig these things out?"

"This whole meadow will be excavated," said Silenus. "We'll take it down a couple feet. That should do it."

"What will it do?" asked Bert.

Mr. Faunus had explained this to him time and again, but Bert just wasn't getting it. And he had a degree in the natural sciences! If he couldn't understand it, who could?

"This won't mean anything to you," Faunus told him, "but it is our mission to uncover diodes."

"Diodes?" asked Bert.

Faunus had explained to him that diodes were decades away from being conceived and developed – by man – but that they are one-way conductors of energy.

"We have three sets of them here," Faunus told him, surveying the surrounding meadow. "Three sets of two."

Bert couldn't help himself. He did the math in his head and he couldn't avoid having the answer come out to 666. As a young man who had grown up in a strict Protestant household, where fear of Satan was the first thing on the menu every day, the numerology unsettled him. He was already flushed with guilt over having become Mister Faunus' fuck boy and this number thing didn't help to ease his concerns.

"What are we trying to do here?" Bert asked, looking around at the volume of dirt that Faunus was suggesting be moved. "Is it just you and me? This will take a year to dig this out."

"It will be the year that changes your life, young man," Mister Faunus told him, and then he handed him a shovel.

Silenus Faunus had no intention of doing the hard work himself. That's what young Bert was for. Faunus had pumped him full of his special energy and his young charge had grown strong as a bull as a result. He was literally primed for digging.

*

It would take Bert Grimfold nine months to excavate the area, until finally six rounded altar stones were revealed.

When it was done, Bert asked Mister Faunus – "So what happens now?"

"That's on you, young man," Faunus told him. "We need to find someone to care for this property. We need a buyer, a mother."

And with that announcement, Bert Grimfold became a realtor. It is all he would ever become, his natural sciences degree aside. He opened a real estate office in Grass Valley, and he made his first sale, selling the Goat Farm to a family who was moving to the Sierras from their farm in the San Joaquin Valley.

For some reason, it was emphasized to Bert Grimfold that the buyer for the property must be someone committed to using the property for the raising of goats, and it must be a woman.

A metal entry gate was created announcing entry into the "Goat Farm".

Over the years, the property passed through many hands, and Bert handled all those real estate transactions, always making certain that the property would be maintained as it was designed to be – a place where goats grew, matured, and entered the world. In every case, the money for the transaction came from women, all married, most of whom had come into their stakes through inheritances. They were always older, stable women, who thought of the property as the place they would spend the rest of their lives. In that, none were disappointed.

Selling real estate was never the career that Bert Grimfold wanted, but he never got the chance to work as a mining engineer. Nobody would have him or take him seriously. He wasn't a mining engineer, but rather was this creepy homosexual whose only source of income seemed to be the selling and reselling of this weird property south of town.

Bert grew old and isolated, and one day the authorities came calling to investigate his business, which had never been properly licensed by the state of California. His office was shut down and Bert seemed to disappear from history until one day he got a message of some kind – a telepathic alert – that his last buyer, Mrs. Breedlove, was running out of gas. She was old, her husband had been lost, and she just couldn't keep up with the maintenance of the Goat Farm any longer. She had lost her mind and become an empty shell, which was a far cry from the lady she had been when he sold her the property.

Lita had been quite the looker. She had been a mature woman, well into middle age when she took over the Goat Farm, but that's what the place required – a mother presence, one whose temperature ran hot.

Lita had been a great goat mistress in the beginning. She did everything she was called upon to do. She allowed herself to be taken by the forest stranger, and she had learned to like and even yearn for his carnal attentions. And as their relationship grew, and as Lita's husband disappeared, the Goat Farm flourished. Somehow the place became filled with billys and nannys and they had many kids, and for years Lita exploited them for their produce and their grazing proclivities. Those were the good years in Nevada County and all around. She would rent her goats out to surrounding locales, who prized them for their efficiency in reducing heavy undergrowth to close-cropped grass.

Then, one day, the forest stranger stopped coming to the meadow and Lita was left alone and the place started to die.

That is when Bert Grimfold showed up, unannounced on the Goat Farm. He was old. In fact, he was supernaturally old. Part of the deal he made with Mister Faunus was that he would be supplied with the energy required to do the job he was chosen to do. He didn't know that it would go on forever – that he would continue to age, and whither, but he would not die, for the Goat Farm could not survive without him. He was tasked with supplying fresh flesh, keeping the place going forever.

"It's time to let it go, Lita," Bert told her.

He found her standing out on the deck overlooking the lagoon, staring blankly into space, a burned-out shell of the person she had been.

She felt his presence, but she didn't bother to look at him. She knew what he was here to say.

She felt such shame. Her poor kids had all turned mutant and she had become a monster of filicide.

"There is a woman from the Bay Area," said Bert, "and she'll buy the farm, take it off your hands. She doesn't know she's coming yet, but she'll do a good job, Lita. She'll bring it all back, make it what it once was."

And with that Lita's heart was fully broken, and her spirit became fully dead.

Bert Grimfold recognized that, but he had one more task that she must accomplish before she could be freed of the obligations she had made.

He told her that he needed for her to find the skull of a large goat – one with horns still attached.

"I need for you to find such a skull and paint it with heavy red lacquer, so that it shines," Bert told her. "Hang it someplace in your house. That's all it will take and then you'll be done. Then you'll be able to rest, my dear."

CHAPTER 44

You never get a call in the night that is a call you want. No agent ever calls you at 3 a.m. to tell you that he has sold your book. The Publisher's Clearing House people never knock on your day in the middle of the night to give you a giant check. To the contrary, it's usually a Highway Patrol officer asking if you are the father or son of somebody, or its your dad calling to tell you your mother has died.

Ben knew immediately what it was going to be when his cell phone vibrated. It was 3:33 a.m., which Ben noted as important because there was a part of him that believed in absolutely everything, including numerology.

His father had passed.

The call came from Ben's stepmother, who was delirious. She had awakened in the night to the realization that Ben's father, her second husband, was lying beside her cold as stone. He had probably been dead for hours, apparently gone to the afterlife peacefully in his sleep.

Ben listened to his stepmother's anguished account of what she had experienced, and he closed his eyes in thanks. To himself he thought, bless Dad's heart. That's the way he should have gone, peacefully in his sleep.

The man had been an angel, an evolved spirit in Ben's mind, and his father's generosity and supportive nature had molded Ben's approach to life. He had hated that his decision, all those years ago, to leave his native grounds for California had robbed him of time with his parents.

His mother had died six years earlier, and Ben had never recovered from her loss. He had lived in daily dread of the day when the call would come that his father, too, was gone, and that he was orphaned in life. At least he had Joanna, who was also without her parents, now.

Ben knew the call would create a fracas. Joanna would resist a trip to Ben's family home, in the Midwest, as she always had. She had a strong bias against people from all parts of the country outside of California and virtually no patience for standard protocol and etiquette where family matters were concerned.

This had been a point of friction with Ben's family, particularly his mother, who was deeply grounded in etiquette and tradition, which had contributed to an obstinance in Joanna's handling of in-law matters. Ben had made few trips to his home grounds over the years, always going by himself, which inevitably yielded a raft of questions about why his wife had not accompanied him.

She owed Ben this trip. She could at least deign to attend his father's funeral, as she had his mother's.

Joanna took the news hard. She had truly loved Ben's Dad, as did everyone, and losing him was a loss to her, taking down the last parental figure she and Ben had.

She knew that Ben was crushed, because she had seen the changes that came over him when he lost his mother. A connection to his past was lost, and he had begun to float in perceptible ways. He had stopped caring, in many ways, about life and even about Joanna.

He cared about his Dad, who he thought about obsessively; practically the only thing he thought about outside of his writing and his weird obsessions with aliens and cryptids. And now that part of Ben's life would be gone, and Joanna knew how this would float him even further from reality, which to him was a painful place that he had always sought to avoid by writing a different one for himself.

"We make reality up as we go," he told Joanna, and he really believed that.

But the reality was that Ben's father was gone, and so Ben and Joanna did the thing Ben hated most. He flew. They drove to the airport in Sacramento and got on a plane to Kansas. And so, for a few days, the Goat Farm was left on its own.

212

CHAPTER 45

Guita couldn't help herself.

The minute she received a call from Joanna, telling her that she and Ben were on their way to a funeral in Kansas, she started making a list of things to do. Joanna would need direction – she was lost without it – and Guita was full of that type of thing.

In fairness, Guita was that way with everybody: a life coach.

She and Joanna were part of a group of eight friends who had known each other since high school. They all remained in the San Francisco Bay Area and so went through life together.

The identifying trait shared by this large group of friends was that they were remarkably non-judgmental with one another, except for Guita, and they cut her slack for her improprieties. It would have been difficult for an outsider to understand why she had been granted this unique leeway to be a mean girl among naïfs, though Joanna had really championed it. She knew that Guita was hurt inside in ways that could never be mended, and so she cajoled the others to go easy on Guita, who she felt had a good heart and the best of intentions.

Guita made lists of peoples' shortcomings.

In fact, it was common conversation among their group that Guita had each of them categorized, like icons for personality types, and she had plans for the improvement of each. They all ended with all her friends coming to live in some mythical retreat that she envisioned building on her property. Guita was rich so could realistically imagine such things. There they would all live under her governorship, because Guita knew what was best for each of them. She had it all worked out.

The fucking Goat Farm stuck in Guita's craw. It ruined everything. It took her beloved Joanna – the brightest of the "seven sisters" as they called themselves, Guita being a slightly older sister who graduated high school before the others came up with their club name – out of her orbit and influence. Not officially being a "sister" had contributed to a lifelong fear in Guita of being left out of things, and she now felt that Joanna had dumped her for this bizarre property in the Sierras, which was incomprehensible to her.

The minute she learned that Ben and Joanna were going to be away from the place for a few days, Guita convinced herself that it was absolutely necessary that she safekeep the property in their absence.

She didn't tell Joanna of her plan, but Joanna had pointed out to her where she kept a key to the front door – beneath a welcome matt that read "California Living" – and so Guita knew how to let herself in.

Ben and Joanna left on a Monday, and by 10 a.m. the next day Guita had completed the two-hour drive from the Bay Area and was headed up the rutted dirt road to the Goat Farm.

She moved cautiously ahead through the forest, moving slowly along in her low-slung Lexus.

Guita watched the trees like a hawk, looking for movement, which she found in abundance, which delighted her. She was nuts for creatures of all kinds. She always had the best-trained dogs and she was an adopter of abandoned pets. She typically had cages around her house with big floppy-eared rabbits that she'd rescued from classrooms, and sometimes even wilder critters, like racoon.

As she approached the turn-in to Cooter Riley's property, Cooter's Alsatians charged down the drive and toward her car.

Then they suddenly skidded to a stop and stood in silent amazement.

Guita had brought her car to a stop and rolled the window down to talk with them.

"Hi, guys! Aren't you big and beautiful? How are you doing today?" she said, leaning out the window as the two giant dogs looked at her bewildered. "Come here," she said, reaching out the window and motioning with her hands.

The two started nervously dancing in place, glancing at each other as if neither knew what to make of this Die Hexe. They whimpered and moaned, seemingly caught in a mixture of canine emotions, torn between wanting to be the protectors they were trained to be and pups still yearning for mom.

"Come here," Guita purred, as seductively as Guita could purr, and little-by-little one of the dogs moved closer, holding his head low in a submissive posture. It was like he was being commanded by some primal force that he recognized and to which he bowed in obeisance.

"There you go."

Guita gently touched the top of the first dog's head, and he raised his muzzle so she could scratch under his chin. And seeing that, the other dog moved cautiously toward the car, sniffing the air, smelling Guita to see that she was not foul and could be trusted. And then he was at the side of the car, using his head to push the other dog out of the way, competing for Guita's attention, reveling in her touch and her comforting voice. She had this tone she had developed through years of working with special education students, which to a standard-issue person sounded extraordinarily condescending, but it apparently charmed dogs.

This mid-road love making went on for a full five minutes, before Guita apologized and explained that she had to go.

"You guys go back home now, stay out of the road," she cautioned, as if there was any chance that these giant dogs were going to be struck by vehicles speeding by. Most vehicles moving up this road were in danger of being struck by them, but not Guita. For reasons only the universe can understand, she befriended Cooter Riley's hell hounds and then went on her merry way to be astonished all over again by the Goat Farm.

*

Guita opened the big metal gate to the property, and then drove on in. This time, she didn't stop under that big oak that made a roundabout of the dirt area in front of Joanna's house. She remembered too-well that incident with the black snake, so instead of parking in the shade of the tree, which seemed to her like the obvious thing to do, she pulled in over by where Joanna had left her Mercedes, parked at the feet of the Kali sculpture.

Guita pulled her car to a halt and then got out and stood beside her car, staring up at the Hindu goddess, radiant as rusted metal can be in the purifying morning sun.

Kali looked down on her with suspicion.

Guita looked around the farm, surveilling the place with her eyes and making mental notes of her responses to what she was seeing.

It looked to her like a rundown mess, and that observation ignited Guita's interest in the place.

She would completely remake it, if it were hers. In fact, as she looked around at the paddocks, the barn, the lagoon with the mysterious island, and the French farmhouse, in her favorite color blue, she was overwhelmed with envy of Joanna.

Joanna could have something like this, because she had Ben – a partner in life – where Guita was on her own. Her whole life had been a series of disastrous long-term relationships. She would cycle through egomaniacal, delusional alcoholics every seven years or so, usually surrendering huge sums of money along the way. She didn't trust men at all, not even Joanna's Ben, who she could hardly stand. And the thought that Joanna had abandoned her in the Bay Area, with Ben, and now had all this, when she wasn't even an ani-

216

mal lover, felt like an egregious injustice committed against her by the universe. It just wasn't fair, because she would know just what to do with the Goat Farm if it was hers.

Guita walked across the yard to the path that led down to the lagoon and then down to the deck, where she stood for a while, looking into the water.

It was peaceful. The air was soft and mild, a gentle breeze carrying the fragrances of sweet nectars. Frogs made their odd, other dimensional sounds, and birds chirped. A crow flew overhead, scolding her as he passed by, disappearing off into the trees. There were honeybees everywhere, alighting on the colorful flowers that grew naturally all over the area. A bushy-tailed gray squirrel hopped over near where she stood and stared at her intently.

"Hello", she said.

The squirrel didn't say anything, just looked at her a few moments longer before going on about his day, hopping off into the weeds.

Guita filled her lungs with the fresh air that gave the entire farm a special quality, as if things were rich and pure here, filled with nutrients outside the normal range. There was a magic sense about it, a place of regeneration and healing.

There her spirits fell.

She had lost any sense of the promise of regeneration on any level, or the possibility of feeling well. She had no sense that any of that was within her grasp, for she doubted it ever had been. It was as if she had been born under a certain star cluster that bound her to days of torture and disillusionment and delighted in her pain. And now she was old, and after decades of orientation she was altered and unable to be freed, though she had mapped out every strategy imaginable. She hadn't tried other than the disastrous options that she then just kept repeating.

Guita wandered from the deck by the lagoon and walked to the front door of the house. There she pulled back the "California

Living" matt and found the key to the door. She opened it and let herself inside.

Joanna had done a lot with it since Guita had been here before. The arrangement of the room was charming, incorporating all of Joanna's familiar antique furnishings, some of which had been gifts from their big group of friends.

But there among the familiar furnishings and paintings were others that Guita had never seen before: strange works of art that were occult in nature and depicting the paranormal.

Then she saw the enameled red horned-skull, and hanging right next to it was Joanna's creation, which she called the "Whore of Baphomet".

It was unsettling to Guita. Joanna had always enjoyed the macabre. She loved visiting haunted places and told convincing stories about her own strange experiences with precognition and astral travel. Guita did not share Joanna's fascination with horror novels and bloody cinéma vérité. She didn't even feel comfortable with Joanna's outré taste in modern music, so staring at these painted skulls, one adorned like it was a grim artifact from a Satanic wedding ceremony, sent shivers down her spine.

What was her friend becoming? And more to the point, what could be done to bring her back to her old self, to normal?

"What are you doing here?"

Guita startled and turned quickly to see Willie, the boy Joanna had met in the meadow.

"Get away from me," said Guita, backing away, scrambling for her purse in which she carried mace.

"What are you doing in Joanna's house?" asked Willie, with a vocal inflection weighted with suspicion and challenge. He had a mischievous quality, a dangerous nature.

"I am a friend of Joanna's," said Guita. "Who are you?"

"I live here," said Willie.

Guita frowned. "Where?"

"Here," said Willie. "You are in my home."

Guita found her mace and held it up in front of her, pointing it threateningly at Willie. "What the fuck are you talking about? Joanna and her husband Ben live here. They are friends of mine."

Willie smiled in an ornery way, baring teeth that looked like they hadn't been brushed in a long time, if ever. "Joanna isn't here."

"I know that," said Guita, "So what are you doing here?" She held her mace with considerably greater confidence than Ben had held his bear spray. It created a sense that she had practiced for this moment, something Ben had failed to do.

"You like those dogs, don't you?" said Willie.

Guita looked at him with uncertainty. "What are you talking about?" she asked, keeping her mace trained on Willie's face.

"That guy Cooter, with the big dogs, who lives up the road," said Willie. "I saw you talking to them and petting them."

"Where were you?" asked Guita, taken aback.

"Nearby," said Willie. "I'm not afraid of those dogs, they can't catch me."

"What are you doing on this property?" asked Guita.

"I told you, I live here!" said Willie.

"What's with coming into Joanna's house?" asked Guita, the inflection in her voice telling Willie that she was here with the authority to remove him from the premises.

"I'm watching over things," said Willie.

"Well, thanks, but we don't need that," said Guita. "I'm here now and I think you should leave. Go back to wherever you live."

"I told you," said Willie, "this is where I live."

Guita was growing agitated with his obfuscations, as well as her growing sense that he had been watching her from the time she pulled onto the road to the Goat Farm. How could that even be? How could this hick kid, who wasn't even wearing shoes, get from the next farm property, where the German Shepherds lived, all the way to Joanna's place. That it seemed impossible, unless he had a vehicle stowed someplace out of sight, gave her a creepy feeling. What was going on here?

"Look," said Guita, "I am going to be here in Joanna's absence, and I don't know who you are…"

"Willie – my name is Willie."

"I don't believe Joanna gave you any permission to come into her home, and I want you to leave before I feel the need to call the authorities."

"I saw you in the meadow," said Willie.

Guita froze. "What do you mean?"

"You were here once before, with Joanna, and I saw you out in the meadow," said Willie.

Guita winced and her eyes fluttered.

"You're fat, that's why Veebo didn't come and fuck you like he does Joanna," said Willie. "He fucks her all the time, or at least he used to until she beat him up. He wouldn't fuck you, though."

Guita's eyes flashed with anger, and a touch of shame. "Get the fuck out of here, right now! You little bastard!" And with that torrent, she let fly a cloud of mace, which caused Willie to turn and exit quickly through the open door, coughing and gagging as he went.

That smell still lingered when Ben and Joanna returned to their home three days later.

Joanna had no idea that Guita had visited. She tried to call her when she got unpacked, to tell her about the funeral and how it all went, but all she could get was an answering machine.

Guita would get that way. Sometimes she would just get upset about something and neither Joanna nor any of the other Seven Sisters would hear from her for months. And they would know that Guita was hurt, in some way, and had retreated to lick her wounds.

She had the kind that never heal and that occasionally made it hard for her to face another day.

CHAPTER 46

Joanna walked out into the stone meadow and there she found Willie, waiting for her.

"Where have you been?" he asked.

"What are you doing here?" asked Joanna.

"I saw your friend in your house," said Willie.

Joanna frowned. "What friend?"

"The one Veebo wouldn't do sex with," said Willie. "Do you have others?"

"Guita was here?" asked Joanna.

"Is that her name?" asked Willie, quizzically. "What kind of a name is that?"

"What was she doing?" asked Joanna.

"That's what I wanted to know," said Willie. "So, I asked her. I said, what are you doing in Joanna's house?"

Joanna looked at him for a moment, considering the scene he was describing.

"And what did she say?" asked Joanna.

"She sprayed me with something that burned my eyes and so I ran away," said Willie.

Joanna shook her head. "That sounds like Guita."

"I can see why Veebo wouldn't do sex with her," said Willie.

"Does she do that to everybody?"

Joanna shook her head. "She doesn't care that much for men."

"You do though, don't you," said Willie. "You like to do the sex."

Joanna could feel the meadow working its magic on her. She was becoming light-headed, a little disoriented, and she steadied herself by placing one hand on the altar rock on which Willie was sitting.

"You are starting to feel it, aren't you?" asked Willie.

Joanna just looked at him, floating in her mind.

"The old woman used to take her clothes off and come and lay down on one of these rocks, waiting for someone to show up and do sex with her," said Willie.

"What do you mean, someone to show up?" asked Joanna. "Wasn't it Veebo?"

"Veebo and the others," said Willie.

"The others?"

"Yeah," said Willie.

"Like Veebo?"

"Veebo's an idiot," said Willie, shaking his as if in disbelief.

"Like Veebo, Willie?" asked Joanna, with more urgency in her voice. "Are you saying there are others like Veebo?"

Willie looked at her like she was the stupidest thing in the meadow. "They're everywhere," said Willie. "They are everywhere, doing sex with all kinds of people. It's only Veebo whose left here. He's too stupid to be anywhere else."

Joanna sat down on the altar, overcome with dizziness and disorientation. She lay back flat and looked up into the blue sky.

"These are your brothers?" confirmed Joanna.

"Yep," said Willie.

"Do the others ever come, here I mean?"

"If you want them to," said Willie.

"You say they are different from Veebo?"

"They are smarter than Veebo but all they want to do is have sex all the time, just the same," said Willie.

"Do they look like Veebo?"

"Some are bigger and stronger, prettier," said Willie. "They are all horny, like you."

"What do you mean – and I'm not horny," said Joanna. She hadn't realized that the whole time she was laying on the altar that she was unconsciously removing her clothing.

"You are beautiful," said Willie, sitting next to her, admiring her naked form. "Would you like for me to fuck you?"

Joanna was no longer in command of her senses, or even her tongue. "Shut up, your just a kid," she said, her eyes lingering on his for a long moment, then moving down his body.

"I never see you do sex with Ben," said Willie.

"We don't do sex anymore," said Joanna.

"Why?" asked Willie.

"He isn't interested anymore," said Joanna. "Ben's old."

"He isn't well," said Willie.

Joanna frowned and looked at him. "What do you mean?"

"I don't know, I think it's supposed to be that way. There is something wrong with the men who come here," said Willie. "They never last long, and then they go."

"Where?" asked Joanna. "Where do they go?"

Willie shrugged. "I don't know, down below where the goblins go. The fauns know. They do all that."

"Who are the fauns?" asked Joanna.

"You've seen them," said Willie, "out on the island."

"You mean the lagoon?" asked Joanna.

"Yeah," said Willie. "I know you've seen them."

"You seem to know a lot," said Joanna. "I've seen girls on that island..."

"Fauns," corrected Willie.

Joanna looked at him and frowned. Willie looked like a boy, anyone would have thought as much. He was strange, with his odd, puckish features, but Joanna had never once thought of him as other than human. Those girls who she had seen on the island in the lagoon - they were something else. She glanced down at Willie's bare feet, which were topped by a tuft of curly light hair but were otherwise no different from hers. That wasn't what she had seen of those girls on the island. They had hooves, at least that's what she thought she had seen.

"Why don't they look like you, Willie?" asked Joanna.

"I'm not a faun," said Willie.

"What the fuck are you?" asked Joanna.

"What am I?"

"Are these girls you call the fauns your sisters?" asked Joanna.

"No," said Willie, shaking his head, like the thought tasted bad.

"Where do they come from?" pressed Joanna.

Willie shook his head. "I don't know," he said. "Down below, I think."

Joanna stared at Willie for a long moment, trying to comprehend his strange nature. He was just a boy in almost every sense, and yet was clearly an *Other*, as exotic as his idiot brother, the rapist. He just hadn't turned buck yet. Then her thoughts went to the girls in the lagoon - the fauns, as Willie called them.

"What does that mean, Willie? What do you mean, down below?"

Willie shook his head. "I don't know, sometimes they are here
and sometimes they aren't. They belong to this place, but I think
they go deep down someplace. Things happen when they come
back."

Joanna frowned. "What do you mean things happen?"

"The men," said Willie. "They always take them under."

"But I don't understand, you told me this place - the Goat Farm
- is your home," said Joanna. "The first time we met, you told me it
was more your home than mine."

She stopped for a moment, exasperated at her inability to get an
answer out of Willie that she could understand. She stared at him
hoping he would volunteer something.

Willie could tell she was asking him something, but he couldn't
understand what it was.

"When you leave the meadow, Willie, where do you go?" asked
Joanna.

Willie seemed baffled by the question. "Home to the trees, I
guess," said Willie.

"To your parents?" asked Joanna. "What about your parents?
Where are they?"

"My parents?" asked Willie, perplexed. "I don't know what you
are asking me. I just hear you, here in the meadow."

"What do you mean, you hear me?"

"I guess you were just thinking about me," said Willie.

"And so you just showed up?" asked Joanna.

"I heard you a long time ago and I've been waiting, and then
you came."

"And your idiot brother?" asked Joanna. "Did he know I was

coming, too?"

"I don't know," said Willie. "You might have thought about him."

"Why would I think about him?" asked Joanna.

"I don't know," said Willie, shaking is head and grinning, "but he was here. You know that."

"Yeah," said Joanna, shaking her head sadly. She knew that.

What must she have been thinking?

CHAPTER 47

Joanna was sitting on the deck, staring into the lagoon, when she heard the girls at the gate. There were eight of them.

"Hello," one yelled. "We are from UC-Davis and wondered if we could talk with you about your property."

Inside, Ben heard the voices, while typing away at his laptop, and he stopped to listen. He heard Joanna yell – "Hold on a second, I'll get the gate."

That prompted him to rise from his chair and go out to the living room, where the windowed wall gave him a clear view of the entry. He saw Joanna walking briskly across the yard toward where they were gathered, standing outside a minivan.

They had a brunette spokesperson who introduced herself with a handshake, after Joanna swung the gate open. "Hi, my name is Gina – and this is Tara, and Dawn, and Clarice, and Starlight, and Tina, and Georgie, and Elizabeth."

They were adorable, all between eighteen and nineteen years of age, all shapes and sizes, and all lit up like lightbulbs with expectation of what they had come to see.

"We all go to school at UC-Davis and are students of Dr. Jones, and he told one of our group about the stones in your meadow," explained Gina, ever so carefully. She had every hope that the owners of the Goat Farm would be as nice as Dr. Jones had said they were, but there was also every chance that they may not be welcomed, or even be rudely turned away.

"What did Dr. Jones tell you?" asked Joanna.

Gina thought for a moment, then giggled and looked at another of the girls. "I don't know – Tina, do you want to say?"

Tina was a blond princess, though apparently not of the virgin variety. "Dr. Jones and I are lovers," she confided, intuitively sensing that she could speak candidly to Joanna, another woman. The admission sent a burst of giggles exploding through the entire group and Tina turned a rosy red color.

Joanna picked up on her blush immediately and sought to capitalize. "Ah, does he ever mention horny goat weed?"

And with that the whole pack exploded in a laughter so boisterous that it brought Ben out onto the porch to see what was happening.

"That's our name for him!" Gina cried. "Horny goat weed!" And again the octet rang with laughter, thrilled at being young and completely unaware.

Joanna was laughing hard herself, thrilled that the horny goat weed reference had scored so high on the resonance scale. "That Tom Jones," she thought, sending a silent nod of credit to that man to whom credit was due. It wasn't every archaeologist who boasted his own coven.

"We are Wiccans," Gina explained, as the laughter subsided. "And Horny Goat Weed told Tina…"

"I wish you wouldn't call him that," complained Tina, to no response.

"…about a meadow on your property where there are six glowing altar stones. And we came hoping that you might let us see it – the meadow and the stones."

Joanna looked skeptical. "And is your interest as archaeology students at the university, or as Wiccans?"

The girls exchanged glances, before Gina spoke for them as a group. "Wiccans," she said.

*

Joanna left them standing at the gate while she went up to the porch to talk with Ben.

"What is this about?" he asked.

"College kids," said Joanna. "They found out about the stone meadow from Horny Goat Weed."

"What?" asked Ben.

"Dr. Jones, the family archaeologist," said Joanna. "He's been fucking Tina, the tall blonde who looks like she is about to inherit money."

Ben looked from Joanna over to the gaggle of Wiccans. "You found out all this just talking there at the gate? So what do they want?"

"They didn't say," said Joanna, "but my guess is that they want to do some ritual out there in the moonlight."

That raised Ben's eyebrows. "Wow, that's a gas. Can we watch?"

"Are you good with the insurance risks?" asked Joanna. "If anything happens to them on our property, after we gave them permission to be on it, we stand liable for whatever damages may accrue."

"Have you been reading law journals or something?" asked Ben.

"Just making cautious assumptions," said Joanna. "We have known of that meadow to have interesting effects on people."

Ben was looking over at the girls with a wry smile on his face. "What's the worst that can happen?" he asked.

*

It was soon revealed that the girls had quite an evening in mind, complete with pagan reveries and ritual magic. They had arrived with the expectation of acceptance and had brought with them everything they would need to get through the evening. Their plan was to rehearse their rituals and dine on sandwiches and salads they had picked up from Panera. Joanna had set them up on the redwood deck above the lagoon, and lighted tiki torches that were positioned around the platform in a way that serviced the scene spectacularly. They looked like vestal virgins in the light of the torches and the moon overhead. Joanna and Ben could hear them practicing incantations, refining their pitches in anticipation of a night they would never forget – that is, if Dr. Jones had been telling the truth about the meadow, and the stones. He had been cheating on Tina of late, though she was the only one of them who didn't seem to know about it. They were planning on using this night to break the news. Horny Goat Weed had been her first man.

Just after midnight, the eight girls stripped down to their underwear and then donned red capes, so they all looked like Little Red Riding Hood, and they each had little red slippers. Then, carrying two tote bags filled with candles, incense, scrying balls, tarot cards, pendulums, spell-casting supplies, wands, gemstones, and a black kettle, they made their way out to the meadow.

Once there, they set about the task of setting their scene, placing candles on the altar stones, all contained in glass in such a way that it protected their flames, and in the middle they laid out a blanket with a large pentagram embroidered onto it, and there they laid out the fetishes of their pagan craft.

Those tasks had not been fully accomplished when each of the girls began to report disorientation, to feel dizzy.

"It is nature, speaking through the rocks, the trees, the grass, and light of the moon," instructed Gina sagely. "Feel the energy they give you and let it flow through you."

And so they fell into a swaying motion, an unspoken ritual movement not inspired by anything they had rehearsed, but rather by the night itself. There was a beat, a rhythm that was growing, an electricity they could all feel as rhythmic bursts.

It hit them first in their olfactory senses, an aroma that swelled up around them and made them feel dreamy and soft. And then there was a soft humming in their ears, that had a subtle variation, like the sounds of cicadas, accented by the occasional chaw-chaw-chaw of tiny finger cymbals, like little dancing spirits, just letting them know they were there, in their heads.

Then the pulsing sensation began to move the fluids within their bodies, putting them in a gentle wash of stirring impulses, and a growing sense that some force or energy was moving down their spines, wrapping around their hips, and slipping between their legs. There was a throbbing.

The girls had not even begun a single exercise and already they were caught in the grip of something, swaying like cobras around their portable pentagram, moving without conscious thought of themselves or any of the others. There was something else in their minds, hungry and coming for them, and this dance they were doing was for him, or her, or whatever it was going to be. It was out there, they could feel it, and it did not feel like danger so much as it felt like an approaching edge, a rip in the governance of human expression, and they were poised to dive into that void.

At three o'clock that morning, when the moon was high in the sky and marshaling the shadows of night to keep its secrets from being revealed, the stones began to glow.

It was the blue ray, that sapphire light that brings forth magical things, that Buddhists believe produces peace of mind, equanimity, and chases away evil thoughts by creating a proper balance of energies within one's circulatory system. The blue ray, they say, opens doors for the spirit of man.

And forth they did come.

*

The girls emerged from the meadow at sunrise the next morning.

Joanna had stayed up all night, worrying for them, for she knew full well what would happen in that meadow. She didn't understand how Guita got left out of the fun, but she knew those young girls were destined for change, and she had let them go anyway. No one was going to get hurt, that was her calculation and gamble. She didn't even need to know what had happened back there in the night, she could imagine. She saw the blue ray, lighting up the trees, and she knew what those crazy fucking girls were going to call forth, because they weren't so different from her, and she knew what she had done.

It was really pissing her off that the one that her mind had brought forth was that idiot Veebo, he of the giant, throbbing dong, who as Willie said, would "fuck anything". That had really hurt, and now she was even sharing that moron with these stupid, silly girls. Was there no fantasy out there left to be her own?

"So, how was it?" Joanna asked as the girls made their way, like a string of prisoners, through the paddock areas and back to the turnaround, where she waited by their parked van.

They passed by her, one by one, looking straight ahead and not saying a thing, finding it easier to just get in the van and get the hell out of there than to explain anything about their experience. They could tell by the way she looked and acted that she knew anyway. That bitch had probably been back there herself and knowing what she knew she had sent them back there to live out their wildest fantasies. That is just what happened within the context of their pagan fascinations. They got just the strange ritual experience they sought, and now they were changed, exhausted, and they just wanted to go home.

"So, what are you going to tell Horny Goat Weed?" chided Joanna, glancing at Tina, who glanced back for a fleeting second, before returning her gaze straight ahead. "Are you going to tell him that the stones glowed for you?"

One of them pulled the sliding side door shut and without saying a word, they drove away from the Goat Farm, their curiosities satisfied, their fantasies at least for the moment fulfilled.

The Goat Farm

CHAPTER 48

Joanna looked at the meadow around her, at the forest, its dark recesses just a stone's throw away, and at the barn and the stables in the distance. The sky was blue, just an occasional puff of white cloud passing slowly overhead, like gentle entities watching over the landscape below. The air was fresh, fragrant with blossoming flowers.

"Everything here has to be special," she said, not certain the words hadn't only been a thought in her mind.

Somehow Willie heard it.

He seemed to come out of nowhere - she hadn't been aware that he was there, though she had become used to this about him. He showed up with the thoughts that crossed her mind.

Willie frowned, like what she was saying didn't make any sense. "It is special," he said, as if speaking the obvious. "I don't think anyone but you can make anything like this."

"What do you mean?" asked Joanna.

"I think it's called magic?" said Willie.

"I can't do magic, Willie," said Joanna. "I'm not even sure how Ben and I are going to support ourselves here. We put everything I owned – we owned – into buying this place. Now all Ben wants to do is write his stupid book, which means we'll run out of cash soon. Then I could use some magic."

"Don't worry, Joanna - everything is going to be fine," said Willie. "You've made it that way."

Willie was right, energy had been reborn into the Goat Farm. The place was repopulating.

Neither Ben nor Joanna could imagine where they were coming from. Whole families of goats seemed to wander from the woods only to take up their places in the pens and paddocks of the Goat Farm. They behaved as if they had been there before, as if they were returning to home turf after time away.

"What are we going to do with them?" Ben asked, alarmed by this sudden boom in animal husbandry responsibilities.

"We'll take care of them," said Joanna. "We have supplies in the barn. We'll use that until we can figure out how to feed and nurture all these animals."

Ben looked at her like she was daft. "They aren't ours! They must have wandered off somebody's property."

Joanna shook her head. "They came out of the woods, Ben. There are no goat farmers back in those trees, it's a forest."

"Well they just didn't fall out of the sky, they must belong to somebody," said Ben. "I can make some calls. Who do you call?"

"They are ours, Ben," said Joanna.

"They are not ours!" countered Ben. "Besides, who wants a bunch of goats?"

"The Goat Farm, Ben," said Joanna in a distant, matter-of-fact way, as if the sense of it all was beginning to take form in some far reach of her mind. "The Goat Farm wants them. They have a purpose of some kind. Something is bringing them here. There is reason somewhere behind it all."

Ben just stared at her, unsure of what to say.

Who had she become?

CHAPTER 49

"You are fucking kidding me!"

Ben, talking to his agent on the phone, sounded alarmed, and it caught Joanna's attention. Her adorned "Whore of Baphomet" skull hung on the wall next to where Ben stood talking.

"Well thanks!" Ben said into the receiver. "Thanks for calling. Thanks for everything!" He ended his call and turned to Joanna. "I can't fucking believe it," he said.

"I can't believe you are talking that way," said Joanna. "Who was that with the phone?"

"That was Gary, my agent," said Ben, as if in disbelief at what he was just told. He leaned back against the kitchen doorjam and held the palms against his forehead, as if trying to keep his head from exploding. "He sold my book, *The Whore of Baphomet*. More than that, it went to auction. It's a million dollars, Joanna! Arkham House paid a million dollars for it! Gary's talking movie rights and sequels. I don't know how much of that we get, but it's a million fucking dollars for a story about a woman who fucks goats!"

Joanna's face turned white. "It's about a woman who fucks goats?"

Ben grinned, pleased with himself. "Well, in a way. She's the *Whore of Baphomet*, after all. You ever seen Baphomet?"

"Not yet," said Joanna, shaking her head.

CHAPTER 50

Ben couldn't sleep. He was too excited.

He had given up on his dreams years earlier. They had once been his lifeblood, virtually the only thing that had ever kept him going.

He had never fit in well in life. This was something of a mystery to those who knew him, because he was a pretty normal guy in almost every way. He had never been wildly eccentric. In fact, had he been characterized by anything it would have been his enigmatic nature. He shared his thoughts, sometimes to a fault, but he hid his feelings. No one, other than Joanna, ever knew him, and she often felt that she didn't know him well. He kept things hid; not things of detriment to anyone, save possibly himself, but the kind of things you'd have to know to ever really understand or appreciate a person.

People didn't really understand or appreciate Ben. They didn't dislike him – except, possibly, for Guita – but rather just didn't think about him. For a guy who tinkered around on the edges of fame, Ben had been invisible.

That was all going to change now.

Ben sat on the front porch, drinking his Carnivor and looking at the darkness all around. Later, in the darkest part of morning, the stone meadow would glow and light the back part of the Goat Farm. But that strange, mystical occurrence, yet to be explained by Ben's professor friends and their cadre of technical specialist, had become a familiar feature that Ben had come to love.

Those six glowing stones had changed his life. He had written what Joanna would call "a crazy fucking story" and somehow it had worked. Somehow, suddenly, people believed in him, showing it in their most profound and honest way – with their money. There was nothing people valued more than money and getting people to part with it in exchange for something he had created was the victory he had waited for his entire life.

Ben felt a deep relaxation settle over him, so great that it even subdued the discomfort he had been feeling in his groin. It was probably cancer, he didn't care. Ben had crossed the finished line and spiked the ball beyond any manner he could have ever imagined.

He would never have written *"The Whore of Baphomet"*, or anything like it, before he and Joanna had come across this strange place, now looming out before him like deep space.

Ben was amazed at the stars.

They blanketed the black sky with mind-boggling complexity. He could see Aquila, Cygnus, Lyra, Sagittarius, and Scorpius. They gleamed at him in bursts of light, like guiding beacons in the blackness.

Ben had provided for his family.

It wasn't the greatest triumph of mankind. His family consisted of just one person, his Joanna. He had provided for Joanna, set her up so that she would never have to worry about her security ever again. She would never have to be afraid, and she should never want for anything.

Joanna had achieved her dream, and Ben had achieved his. He sat drinking his cabernet and feeling completely full of himself. It seemed to him that magic had happened, and he was a happy beneficiary.

Ben downed the last drop of his wine and the alcohol veil fell over him in its usual fashion. Ben never acted drunk, but in fact the first drink always finished him. He would feel like his whole head and body were swimming, and he would become sluggish, drowsy, and start to see things. That's when he always knew that it was time to call it a night.

It was that time. Ben was buzzed and he closed his eyes and laid his head back, resting against the headrest built into the rocker Joanna had installed on the porch. He felt the fresh air fill his lungs, breathing further energy into his dizziness.

His head began to spin.

Ben opened his eyes, leaned forward in the rocker, and shook his head. He was feeling strangely, to the extent that he wondered how well he would do on the stairs up to the bedroom, where Joanna lay reading. He felt like he needed to lie down.

He stood up, a little shaky on his pins, and as he did, he looked over at the lagoon, and he spotted something – something in the water.

"What the hell?" Ben muttered to himself.

There was an object there, just off the deck.

Ben glanced into the living room window, to see if by any chance Joanna was downstairs, and when he saw she wasn't he stood up and stepped off the porch.

The walkway to the lagoon followed the arc of that line of stones that Tom Jones had convinced himself were the rings of Saturn. Ben had found the idea fanciful enough to use it in his book. There was a line of energy, which led to the lagoon and to that floating island.

Ben followed along the trail toward the water, with only moonlight to show his way. The stones paralleling the walk seemed to glow in their own way, enough that as Ben walked carefully toward the lagoon, he kept his eyes on that object in the water.

It looked like a boat, a little rowboat.

Where in the hell did that come from?

Ben looked back at the house, which made him think he was far more drunk than he had imagined. The place seemed a mile away, as if somehow the path he walked down had stretched out into a long, long trail, at the end of which was this French farmhouse, which now seemed so small in the distance.

Ben blinked his eyes.

His house seemed no larger than a postage stamp.

Ben turned back and looked at the water.

It was a damned boat! Where did this boat come from?

Had this thing been lodged in the rich undergrowth that draped over into the water and been hidden there all along?

Ben stepped up onto the deck and looked down at it.

There were oars!

His first thought was that this was the coolest little surprise he had received since learning yesterday that he was a millionaire! Now he had this cool little boat, too? How freaking cool could life get?

Ben was thinking all of these thoughts when suddenly he glanced up at the floating island.

There were eyes – glowing eyes – looking at him from behind the tall grasses growing there. Three sets.

Ben crouched on the deck, squinting to see what was there, across the water.

Were these animals? They had to be, what else could be out there? On that island? And yet they didn't really look like animal eyes. They didn't glow red, but rather glowed like golden orbs.

"Hello", said Ben, not too loudly. He didn't want to startle any-one.

Was it possible that those crazy girls that Joanna had allowed out into the meadow were back, and had brought a boat with them to get out onto the island?

Ben looked over toward the gate, which was barely visible in the night, but that he could tell was closed. There were no cars in sight, other than he and Joanna's.

How would someone get a boat here?

Ben stared at the island.

The eyes were moving, the glowing orbs blinking on and off as whatever was there moved slowly through the tall grasses.

Then, to Ben's astonishment, they stepped into full view.

It was the fauns, who Joanna had seen but been unable to process. They had to have been a figment of her imagination, but now they were in Ben's mind, too. More than his mind, in plain sight.

There were three of them, dressed most seductively in sheer cloth that did nothing to hide their exquisite forms. Their beauty was so stunning that it made Ben chuckle.

He had to be dreaming. "I must be dreaming," he muttered to himself.

Across the water, standing in the deep grass and staring at him, were iconic forms. There was a blonde-haired girl, and a dark-haired girl, and a red head.

Ben's thoughts immediately flashed to a book he had read once – Jacque Vallee's *Passport to Magonia: From Folklore to Flying Saucers*.

Supernatural forms present themselves in the guise of familiars, of things that make sense for us to see given the borders of our lives, the contexts within which we define our own realities.

Ben was seeing supernatural beings, fauns. He told himself that it wasn't true, that these had to be those screwy UC-Davis coeds back for another round of pop culture role play.

That isn't what he was seeing, though, and he knew it.

These weren't coeds, these were sirens beckoning him toward them, urging him to climb into that little boat and row his way across to them. And he found himself doing it.

Ben found himself acting without free will.

His penis had become erect, to the point that he noticed it. His penis didn't get erect anymore, hadn't in years, but now it had grown so stiff and hard that it felt uncomfortable in his pants.

He lowered himself off the deck and onto the deep grassy area and the edge of the water. There he carefully put one foot inside the boat, which rocked precariously as he allowed his weight, and then the other. The boat rocked back and forth and Ben quickly sat down for fear of tipping it over.

He glanced back behind him at the fauns, and then grabbed the oars he found there and used them to power the little wooden boat away from the bank.

Again, he glanced back at them, not understanding his own behavior but knowing that he had to get to them, even having no thought in his head for what he would do once there. He pushed through the water, and the little boat crossed the forty feet between the shore and the island.

As the boat reached the shore it floated into the overhanging grass, its nose disappearing from sight, and Ben got up and started feeling for land.

He reached out a hand and suddenly realized that one of the girls had reached out and clasped his hand.

It was the red-haired one.

Ben looked at her eyes – strange, golden eyes – and she smiled at him.

He looked down at her skin and saw that it was perfect.

She was soft, unblemished, completely pure.

The blonde faun, and the dark-haired one appeared then, helping him out of the boat.

"Come, come," they said, in voices so sweet with youth that it warmed Ben's heart, and yet as he stepped out of the boat and onto the island it was not his heart that was most on his mind.

They were exquisite.

The fauns were small and beautiful, and Ben stood among them feeling powerful in their presence.

In fact, he had never felt so powerful in is life.

His boner raged.

He felt intoxicated, not just from his beloved Carnivor but from the vibrations he was getting from these girls. These weren't co-eds. Ben had to keep telling himself that there must be a logical explanation for these strange creatures, and he knew rationally that UC-Davis turns out no such products, and yet what could he think?

"Are you real?" Ben asked, completely uncertain of the answer. Was he losing is mind?

"Come, come," said the fauns, and they grabbed his hands and pulled him onto the island, and then further into the tall grasses, into which they all disappeared.

CHAPTER 51

"Ben! Are you out here?"

Joanna had awakened with a start. She had a sudden sense that something had happened to Ben.

It had snapped her out of a most unusual dream.

She had been dreaming that she was in some kind of a primal setting of monolithic stones and priapic imagery. There was fire-light all around her, and flickering shadows. Forms circled about her as she was laid out naked on an altar and an entity of some kind was on top of her, moving within her, fucking her.

He had the eyes of a goat, and horns.

Joanna had snapped out of her dream with the realization that she was having an orgasm. She reached into her pajamas and found she was wet, and she throbbed.

She looked over to where Ben should have been sleeping, but he wasn't there.

Joanna got up from the bed and walked over to the French doors that opened to the balcony, outside, and through the glass she could see the stone meadow, and it was glowing.

It was glowing brighter than she had ever seen it before.

The feeling in her vagina was not like anything she had ever felt before. She was shaking, vibrating, in ways she couldn't stop. She felt thirsty, hungry, desirous.

Joanna pushed her hair back away from her face.

Where was Ben?

She went to the stairway and hollered down. "Ben, are you down there?"

There was no answer.

Joanna walked back over to the balcony doors and looked again over at the stone meadow, which glowed a litmus blue.

Something was happening, something that hadn't happened before, at least not in her experience.

For a long moment, she stared into the distance, into the trees. The stars twinkling outside flashed out to her as they had to Ben, and she recognized it as a signal.

The time was upon her. It was now.

Joanna walked back to the stairway and cautiously made her way down the steps.

Ben was nowhere.

Joanna walked down into the living room and saw that it was empty. "Ben," she called, "where are you?"

When there was no answer, she thought he must be outside, though why he would be at this hour was hard to imagine. She looked through the windows of the living room but couldn't see a thing in the dark night, just the distant glow of the meadow.

She thought to step out onto the front porch, but as she did, she noticed a lighted candle, near the doorway, and she picked it up and carried it with her.

The night was completely still.

Joanna stepped out onto the front porch; her face lighted by the glow of the candle.

"Ben! Are you out here?" said Joanna, not yelling, not willing to break the quiet of night, but rather whispering with some volume.

"Ben's gone, Joanna."

Joanna spun around to see Willie standing close to her.

"What do you mean?" asked Joanna.

"He's gone with the fauns," said Willie. "Don't worry, he's happy and you'll see him again."

Joanna looked from Willie to the lagoon.

"Oh god, no!"

Willie moved close to her, wrapping an arm around her shoulder. The light from the candle lighted their faces and made Willie's eyes glint with fire.

"Don't worry, Joanna," said Willie. "We all love you. More than that, we all need you. Don't you understand? The whole world needs you. It won't go on without you."

"Where is Ben?" asked Joanna.

"Below," said Willie.

And with that the Goat Farm came to life. The goats, which had wandered in great number out of the woods, seemingly from nowhere, now bleated in a noisy chorus from their pens, all facing the house where Joanna stood in the glowing candlelight with Willie.

"It's going to be wonderful, Joanna," said Willie.

The goats bleated in exhortation, beckoning her to believe, to accept that this fate that had been placed upon her was good, and was what she wanted.

"Please, Joanna," said Willie. "He's waiting for you."

Joanna looked at him, eyes wide with terror. "Who is waiting for me?"

"Don't be afraid," said Willie.

He moved behind her and reaching around he gently unbuttoned her pajamas, then pulled the top from her shoulders, letting it fall to the ground, revealing her breasts.

Her beautiful form glistened like an ethereal form in the starlight.

He pulled the bottoms of her Nick and Nora's, dropping them to her ankles, and she stepped out of them without Willie asking.

There she stood in the night, totally naked, lighted only by the Moon, the stars, and the candle she was holding.

With that, Willie walked back to her front side. He smiled at her and then he raised his voice to the heavens and made a sound unlike anything she had ever heard before. It was not human, but rather someting that erupted from deep within her mind that then became Willie's vocalization, his trumpeted bleat.

It was a sound of joy, of relief; a sound intended to announce that change was here.

The Goat Farm went wild with sound, and suddenly there was action everywhere, and light.

Willie vanished from Joanna's side and suddenly sprung up on a lighted pike, standing it straight up with the action of his athleticism, like a pole vaulter leaving his stick upright in the box.

Then suddenly Willie sprung up on another pole to the left side of her, and then another further down the path, and then to the left with another.

Every pole was topped with a fiery torch, so that as each popped up, under Willie's magical mechanics, they created a boulevard of light leading to the stone meadow.

Joanna began to move forward, cautiously stepping along her lighted path.

The ground that had been pitch black at her feet was now clearly visible, beautifully lighted with a purifying light.

She stepped forward, walking slowly, looking all around.

A figure appeared to her right and took the candle from her hand, and then was gone before Joanna saw what it was.

Her naked body shone in the fire light, as she stepped forward, moving slowly, with uncertainty, across the farmyard.

Goats lined up to watch as she passed.

The sculpture of Kali seemed to bow ever so discreetly.

Floating through the air was a sweet sound of young girls singing.

Willie popped up his torches as Joanna moved slowly ahead, moving like nature's child through the night, as if on ritual parade.

The glow from the stone meadow grew in intensity as they approached, until it looked like a rock concert was taking place just on the other side of the dividing line of greenery.

Fireflies filled the air, their little lanterns adorning the night, bringing the stars down to Gaia.

Willie stood at the precipice, waving her to follow, and Joanna obliged.

"Come," said Willie. "Everyone is waiting."

As Joanna reached the wall of tall weeds, Willie parted it for her so she could see beyond, to step into the meadow.

The bleating of goats was everywhere. In the paddocks the billies all mounted the nannys and their amorous engagements electrified the atmosphere.

In the meadow, among the glowing stones, there were faeries, pixies, elves and dwarves. Veebo was there, leering at all of them, and there was another of his kind, perhaps one of his better brothers. He was big and strong, his deltoid and pectoral muscles rippling as he impaled a nymph on one of the altar stones. He was unbelievably beautiful, and as Joanna entered the meadow, he stopped his fornicating and turned his head to look at her.

She wanted him. The feeling overwhelmed her when their eyes

met.

The nymph, who he was fucking, looked over at her and in her eyes was acceptance. She knew her place and would demur to this new queen, this new life force, who she had heard about and had known was coming. She'd been in Joanna's head all along.

They had all been waiting for her, all the characters of her imagination.

The elves and dwarves turned to look at her and the faeries and pixies rushed to meet her.

They flew around her, sometimes darting in to touch her naked skin, curious, as if they rarely had the chance to contact real humans. One landed briefly on a nipple, while another fluttered closely around her vagina, quickly surveilling their new mom.

The faeries gently raised her arms out from her sides and started leading her forward.

The handsome goat boy got up from his intercourse and turned to face her.

What had she become?

She salivated for him – not Veebo, who stood by looking scorned and ashamed, but this new stud whose magnetic gaze clearly messaged his desire for her.

He would be at her soon.

Wetness ran down the insides of her thighs.

"She's here!" announced Willie, and with that he stepped aside.

Out at the front of the property, the metal entryway announcing "The Goat Farm" suddenly topped flames that licked the black night.

In the yard, the metal Kali sculpture moved in slow but perceptible motions, bending in the energy that consumed the entire farm area, bending in reverant honor of the new governess - she who had been promised, who would whip this world into shape.

Rising from the middle of the hexagonal arrangement of altar stones, there stood the lord of this misunderstood world – the world of order from chaos. He was huge, a giant goat-man, with horns like Satan, cloven hooves, a woman's breast, legs covered in ring-leted wool, and a penis the size of the world.

Baphomet.

THE END

256

ABOUT THE AUTHOR

Rick Rice and his family live in California, where he works in the software industry. Other of his books include *ATWOOD: A Toiler's Weird Odyssey of Deliverance, Cooksin - Crime and Redemption in the New West,* and *The Friendly.*